THE FATEFUL SUMMER

THE
FATEFUL
SUMMER

Velda Johnston

DODD, MEAD & COMPANY
NEW YORK

1 2 3 4 5 6 7 8 9 10

Library of Congress Cataloging in Publication Data

Johnston, Velda.
    The fateful summer.

        I. Title.
PS3560.0394F3   813'.54   81-7771
ISBN 0-396-08015-4   AACR2
                                            81003542

To Cousin Emilie Dickey Johnson with love

THE FATEFUL SUMMER

1

How can I convey to you what it was like, that eastern Long Island of my girlhood?

I hear that it has changed so much. That beach where Amanda Dorrance and I strolled that ill-fated June day in 1910, ankles daringly revealed by our walking skirts, is now a "nudie beach," where bare bodies glistening with suntan oil lie stretched on the sand. As for those summer boardinghouses, with long verandas where swings creaked in the warm darkness and mandolin-playing young clerks and salesmen flirted with the daughters of vacationing middle-class families—all those places vanished decades ago.

Many of the twenty- and thirty-room "summer cottages" of the rich remain, though, including the Dorrance house. Protected by its high stone wall, it stands with its wide lawns and caretaker's cottage and tennis court on East Hampton's Goddard Lane. Few people, I imagine, know that on a night nearly three-quarters of a century ago, while an early autumn wind whined around its turreted corners, that big white frame house became the scene of a savage murder.

In fact, perhaps few people even know that it once was called the Dorrance house. It has changed hands a number of times over the years. The present owner, it is said, is a multimillionaire manufacturer from Bombay. Sari-clad women have been seen batting tennis balls about on the clay court where Amanda and I used to play.

To me, of course, all this is hearsay. I have not seen the nude beaches, or the discos and singles bars which, like the boardinghouse verandas of my day, are trysting places of the young. In fact, I have not visited the Hamptons for many years. At my age, the comfort of an air-conditioned Manhattan apartment is preferable to the vagaries of eastern Long Island's summer weather.

But then, this is not my story. It is Amanda Dorrance's story. Even in the bloom of youth, I, Emma Hoffsteader—sandy-haired, and rather too heavy of eyebrows and too slight of chin—was not the sort of stuff of which romantic heroines are made. Amanda, though, could not have escaped the role. Her figure was rounded and yet slender. As we said in those days, a man's two hands could have spanned her waist. In contrast to her blue-black hair—hair long enough to reach almost to that tiny waist when she let it down—her eyes were a deep violet. Her features might have appeared almost too coolly classical if it had not been for the dimples that came and went at the corners of her mouth when she smiled.

But I am sure it was not just her beauty that drew people, especially men, to her. I have known women whose beauty seemed to awe men and to keep all but the most self-confident at a distance. From Amanda, though, one gained an impression of some sort of inner excitement, even wildness. It was a quality that brought the preparatory schoolboys flocking around her at Junior Assemblies. It was a quality that brought a certain look to the face of her girlfriends' fathers. Even my own father, that descendant of solid German burghers, was prone to make a fool of himself in her presence. His eyes would grow brighter, his shoulders would straighten, and he would be apt to refer to some of his dueling exploits as an undergraduate—this, even though he had always said it was distaste for such militaristic nonsense as dueling that had made him bring his young bride from Essen to Brooklyn.

In the usual course of events Amanda and I probably never would have met, at Miss Bradley's School or anywhere else. Miss Bradley's, its classes filled with Potters and Stuyvesants and Auchinclosses, ordinarily would not have welcomed the daughter of a middle-class German immigrant, even one who had prospered modestly as the owner of a chemical-and-dye works. But a business acquaintance of my father's mentioned one day that his aunt was Miss Dorothea Bradley, the school's long-retired founder. My father asked him to use his influence with his aunt to have me, a gawky fourteen-year-old, admitted to the school in the fall.

I don't know why my parents wanted me to attend Miss Bradley's, a school dedicated not to scholarship but to the production of charming debutantes. Perhaps my parents, looking at me through the eyes of love, did not see how unlikely I was to become an ornament of the parlor and ballroom. Or perhaps they—or at least my mother—did see. Perhaps she hoped that I might at least acquire a few social graces, and thus better my chances of making a reasonably good marriage.

Anyway, I became a Miss Bradley pupil that autumn. Each morning, accompanied by one of our two housemaids, I traveled by hansom cab from Brooklyn to the school on Manhattan's East Fifty-fourth Street. In the afternoon the housemaid Tessie would return to the school and accompany me back over the bridge to the Hoffsteader brownstone on a staid Brooklyn street.

I had been at Miss Bradley's less than a month when, one day at noon in the dining room, I saw Amanda Dorrance looking down at her opened algebra text with rebellious distaste. Beginning algebra was the only form of mathematics inflicted upon Miss Bradley's young ladies. Amanda promptly accepted my tentative offer of aid. After that I devoted part of each lunch hour to helping her unmask x, y, and all their elusive company.

Not that Amanda represented the popular cliché, the beautiful nincompoop. She had a good mind, and she used it when she chose to. But she did not exert herself to learn anything that did not interest her. Why should she have? Already it was apparent that hers would be the only kind of feminine success that really counted— that is, the ability to attract highly eligible males. So why should she exert herself to find out what number lurked behind xy-squared?

Before the fall term was over we had become best friends. I began to dine at least once a week at the Dorrances' big marble house on Fifth Avenue, traveling home afterward in the Dorrance carriage. John and Clara Dorrance, far from considering me an unsuitable companion for their daughter, seemed to like me.

Perhaps they considered me sensible. (When you are plain, sandy-haired, and, in your mid-teens, already five feet eight inches tall, you had best cultivate whatever assets you have, including good sense.) Perhaps they also were aware of a reckless streak in their daughter, and hoped that association with me might temper it.

That next summer and for three summers thereafter I spent weeks at a stretch at the Dorrances' East Hampton house, sea bathing, playing tennis, and sailing on the bay in the forty-foot yacht the Dorrances kept moored at Sag Habor. None of the boys who flocked around Amanda during those summers of our growing up showed any sign of falling in love with me, but they seemed to like me well enough.

Was I ever envious of Amanda? Of course I was. But that did not keep me from being fond of her. And it did not make me count myself less lucky to be able to spend my summers on eastern Long Island with its silken beaches, and its warm nights when the pale green glow of fireflies drifted through the trees and above the white-blossomed potato fields.

That unlucky day at the beach when Amanda and Michael Doyle first spoke to each other—I am sure that at times later on even she considered it unlucky—was an especially beautiful one, even for June in the Hamptons. Although the cool temperature had kept the beach almost deserted, the afternoon sun shone brilliantly, and a brisk offshore breeze stirred the curved silvery blades of the dune grass and kicked up whitecaps on the dark blue ocean. Clad in straw sailor hats, big-sleeved blouses, and heavy linen skirts, Amanda and I walked along the firmer sand at the water's edge. At that particular time I was eighteen and three-quarters, and she was a week short of her nineteenth birthday. I know that to everyone, including Amanda and me, it seemed strange that I was the younger, but such was the case.

As we walked, retreating to dry sand now and then to avoid a high-washing wave, we discussed what our futures would be now that our school days were behind us. Amanda seemed to have no plans except to go on enjoying the freedom of her debutante year. (She had made her debut just before Christmas in the Dorrance townhouse. Not only I but my parents had been invited. They were so dazzled by the newly installed electric lights in the crystal chandeliers, and the twelve-piece orchestra, and the masses of flowers, that I had difficulty in persuading my father that I would not want such a coming-out party even if he could afford it. "I would much rather," I said flippantly, "stay in." At which my mother gave a sigh that seemed to say, "Ach, perhaps that would be best.")

And so it was mainly my future we discussed. Miss Farnsworth, the present head of Miss Bradley's, had asked me to come to work in the fall as her assistant. Or, if I chose, I could work in the offices of my father's chemical-and-dye works.

Amanda said, "I should think you'd rather do anything than go back to that silly school." She put her hand on the crown of her sailor hat to steady it. Even though she had anchored it to her thick dark hair with a long pin, it kept threatening to fly away on the brisk breeze.

I nodded. Perhaps I would not choose to spend more time in that semicloistered atmosphere. Perhaps, as my brother would have done if I'd had a brother, I would join the Hoffsteader firm.

"Maybe you're right," I said. "Well, shall we turn back? It's getting awfully windy."

"Oh, let's go on for a while. This is so pleasant."

Pleasant, with the strengthening breeze tugging at our hats and skirts and blowing sand into our faces? I felt a renewal of the suspicion that had come to me an hour ago when, for the third time in a week, she had suggested that we walk along this stretch of beach. She wanted to pass the boardinghouse where twice during the previous week we had seen the dark-haired young man perched on the veranda railing. He had not been visible this week, but I could remember how, on those previous occasions, I had been aware of her eyes sliding toward him in the shadow of her hat brim, and of his gaze fixed upon her. I had been aware, too, of something intangible, a kind of electricity in the air.

I said, "I'm cold."

"Then turn back if you want to. I'm going on for a while."

Not replying, I kept in step beside her. If she, a Dorrance, was determined to parade herself before some anonymous young man in a public boarding-house, then I had best stay with her. Perhaps I could keep her from behaving as foolishly as she otherwise might.

The boardinghouse, built the previous year, stood just ahead of us between two tall dunes. It was perilously close to the water. In fact, about a dozen years later it was smashed and swept out to sea by a howling northeaster. But perhaps its builder had thought that being able to offer seaside accommodations outweighed the risk.

The boardinghouse was in full view now. On its veranda men and women of all ages sat on a row of rocking chairs, chatting or reading or just gazing out at the water. Two shrill-voiced small boys in sailor suits stood on the wooden porch swing, pumping it back and forth.

And the dark-haired young man was there today. In fact, he was coming down the wooden walk toward the sand.

Amanda halted, raised her hand to her head, and shrieked, "Oh! My hat!"

It skimmed through the air and dropped into the water just in front of a low, incoming wave. I was sure that she had raised her hand, not to try to secure her hat, but to loosen the stiletto-like pin that held it.

"I'll get it!"

He ran past us, a tall young man in white flannels and a blue-and-white-striped blazer. Careless of his shoes and trouser legs, he waded into the water, retrieved the hat, and came back to us.

"I'm afraid it's ruined." He held the hat, its broad white band stained, its brim already slightly water-swollen, out to her.

She took it. "It doesn't matter." Somehow she had contrived to lose some hairpins as well as her hat. Several locks of hair, blue-black in the sunlight, had tumbled down around her face. With violet eyes bright and cheeks flushed and dimples playing around her mouth, she had never looked more beautiful.

She added, looking down, "Oh, dear! You're soaked to the knees."

"Well, that doesn't matter either."

I reflected that for a man who probably earned ten dollars a week as somebody's clerk, he was being remarkably nonchalant about the ruin of what might well be his only pair of white flannel trousers.

For the first time she seemed to become aware of her disordered tresses. With a pretty air of embarrassment, she raised her free hand and the one holding her hat to her head. "Good heavens! I've lost some hairpins. I must look a perfect fright."

"Here they are." He bent and picked up several large tortoise-shell hairpins. She handed him her hat and then attempted, despite the breeze that kept blowing her hair across her face, to mend her coiffure.

"Why not go back along the beach to the shelter of that dune up there?" His smiling gaze, moving to me, for the first time acknowledged my presence. "We'll be out of the wind."

And out of the view of his fellow boarders. The veranda sitters were no longer reading or chatting. All eyes were riveted on us.

With him carrying Amanda's hat, as if it were his reason for accompanying us, we walked back along the beach. He said, "My name is Michael Doyle. Michael Terence Doyle, in full."

Irish, I thought. He would have to be Irish.

It seems absurd now, but that was still a time when help-wanted advertisements often warned, "No Irish

9

need apply," a time when even the richest Irish were not welcome in the clubs and drawing rooms of the old-line Yankee aristocracy.

"I'm Amanda Dorrance. And this is Emma Hoffsteader."

Again he smiled at me. He was indeed handsome, I silently acknowledged. His looks were the sort known as "black Irish"—curly dark hair, and eyes of such a dark shade they could almost have been called navy blue. Apparently his nose had been broken at sometime in the past. Its slight irregularity saved his face—square-jawed and high-cheekboned—from the too-perfect handsomeness of young men in the collar advertisements.

Amanda asked, "Are you going to be here all summer?"

"I'm afraid not. My father needs me, or at least says he does."

"Your father?"

"Yes. He's also my boss. I've been working in his office since I got out of Rutgers." After a moment he went on, "My father is Matthew Doyle. He operates bars in Manhattan hotels." He gave the names of three of the city's most expensive hostelries.

So I had been wrong in judging him to be a ten-dollar-a-week clerk. But still, the son of an Irish publican . . .

I looked at Amanda's smiling face in its frame of disordered hair. Obviously his words had not dismayed her. I had a gloomy conviction that at the moment not even the news that his father was a prominent white slaver would have daunted her.

10

We stopped where a dune sheltered us from the wind. He never took his eyes from her as she rolled and twisted lengths of hair and pinned them into place. She asked, "Are you going to be here next week?"

From the way he hesitated I knew that if anyone else had asked that question the answer would have been no. Finally he said, "I'll have to go into town again tomorrow for a few days, but I'll be back out here on Sunday."

"Then perhaps you would like to come to my birthday party next Wednesday night."

I stiffened with shock. He said, "Would I!"

"No presents. I think birthday parties with presents are silly after you grow up. I'll send you a card for the party. You'll have no trouble finding our house. It's on Goddard Lane."

"I'll be there. Will it be evening dress?"

"Yes. My mother is rather a stickler for formality."

"I'll be there," he repeated. He handed her her hat and then said with obvious reluctance, "I must go back now. I promised some people to make a fourth for bridge. But I'll see you Wednesday night. Goodbye, Miss Dorrance, Miss—Miss—"

"Hoffsteader. Goodbye, Mr. Doyle."

Amanda and I turned and walked away. After a few moments I said, "You can't have that man at your party, you simply can't. Send him a note saying that the party has been canceled."

She said with ominous calm, "Why?"

"Because he's Irish, and the son of what your father is sure to call a saloonkeeper. And because you deliberately scraped his acquaintance, the acquaintance of a complete stranger. You know you did."

She ignored the accusation. "I had no idea," she said in a virtuous tone, "that you were so narrow-minded about the Irish."

"I'm not."

And I wasn't. The daughter of immigrants, I could not share the prejudice of many old-line Americans against later arrivals. True, the Germans somehow had managed to be assimilated more quickly than other newcomers. Nevertheless, I had felt the sting of prejudice. When I was a young child, sometimes other children in our Brooklyn neighborhood had called me "kraut." And once I had heard two office employees of my father making fun of his accent.

"And why do you say he's a saloonkeeper's son?" she went on. "His father operates *bars*, bars at the best hotels in New York."

"I'm just telling you what others will say."

I learned then how deeply she was smitten, how determined that no one would keep them away from each other. She said, "You're just jealous! You're jealous because you know he would never have gone into the ocean for your hat, not in a million years."

We had been friends for almost a fourth of our young lives. And in all that time she had never before said such a wounding thing to me.

I did not answer. After a moment she said, head hanging, "I'm sorry. I know that isn't true. I only said it because—" She broke off.

"I know why you said it. But listen, Amanda. You mustn't fall in love with this man. Think what it would do to your parents."

Again she gave me evidence of the recklessness of her feelings. "They are not my real parents!"

I had known that they were not even before Amanda and I became friends. Envious girls at Miss Bradley's, glad that their beautiful classmate bore the faint stigma of adoption, often talked about the mystery of her origins, and speculated to each other about what sort of person her mother had been.

Amanda and I had been friends for nearly a year before she herself told me that the Dorrances were not her natural parents. I recalled how she had looked the afternoon she told me, curled up on the chaise in her pretty room, with its draperies and bed canopy of white eyelet embroidery, in the Dorrances' Fifth Avenue house. Her fifteen-year-old features beneath her pompadour had seemed to grow smaller, as if she shrank from her own words.

After several years of childless marriage, she told me, John and Clara Dorrance had begun arrangements, through a lawyer, to adopt a soon-to-be-born infant. As often happens, no sooner were the arrangements underway than Mrs. Dorrance became pregnant. Nevertheless, she and her husband adhered to their original intention, and adopted Amanda soon after her birth. Thus the Dorrance twins, Lawrence and Lucy—both pale and quiet and in my opinion rather strange—were only about half a year younger than Amanda.

"I don't know who my real parents were," she had told me in a subdued voice. "When I was eight Papa talked to me about it. He said he and Mother didn't know whose child I was. The lawyer had arranged it all,

13

and afterward destroyed his records of the adoption. The lawyer died soon after, so they couldn't have asked him even if they had wanted to. At least, that's what they told me."

Obviously, fifteen-year-old Amanda had wished that the Dorrances were her natural parents. But now, less than four years later, she seemed glad that they were not.

"It would be ridiculous for them to object to Michael Doyle for being Irish. Why, for all anybody knows, my own mother could have been Irish."

What odd prescience made her say that I will never know. But later on, when I met the woman who gave birth to Amanda, I wished that the worst thing that could be said of her was that she belonged to that discriminated-against group.

"Amanda, please. You have to consider your mother and father's feelings. Why, they couldn't love you more if you'd been born to them."

"Maybe that's true of *Papa*."

I remained silent. I long had been aware that Mr. and Mrs. Dorrance differed in their attitudes toward my friend. John Dorrance actually seemed to prefer Amanda to his own children. Perhaps that was why Clara Dorrance's manner toward Amanda had a certain cool, detached quality. Or perhaps she resented the contrast between her healthy adopted daughter and the one born of her body, a girl so delicate that she had been tutored at home rather than enrolled at school.

"Please, Amanda," I said finally, "don't have that man come to your party. No good can come of it."

"Well, I'll think about it."

But as we walked on, with sandpipers skittering ahead of us at the water's edge, I had a glum conviction that on next Wednesday night I would be seeing Michael Terence Doyle.

2

While not exactly avoiding me during the next few days, Amanda nevertheless managed to hold herself somewhat aloof. The morning after our encounter with Michael Doyle, for instance, when I went to her room to suggest that we play tennis, she said that she had letters to answer. I went down the broad staircase to the ground floor, back along a hall to a rear door, and then stepped out onto the lawn.

It was the sort of rare June day the poet Lowell must have had in mind, cloudless as the afternoon before, but warmer, and with only the gentlest of breezes. To my right, inside a high wire fence, was the tennis court, its freshly painted white lines bright in the sunlight. Beyond the court was the greenhouse and beyond that the cutting beds, brilliant with marguerites, salvia, and other annuals. To my left was the white frame cottage occupied by Thorsen, the middle-aged man who in summer acted as head gardener and in winter as caretaker. Straight ahead, at the foot of the sloping lawn, was a small scale replica of part of the garden of Versailles. Classical statues of goddesses and nymphs stood on either side of a long reflecting pool. A flagstone walk stretched before each row of statuary. And between the walks and the pool's edge stood rosebushes laden with white, red, pink, and yellow blossoms. I crossed the lawn and started down the left-hand path, stopping now and then to inhale the fragrance of a rose.

Footsteps behind me on the path. I turned and saw Thorsen. A tall man, with graying blond hair, a sun-browned face, and brilliant blue eyes, he looked more like a seaman than a gardener. "A fine day, Miss Emma."

"Yes. And your roses are beautiful."

He nodded. "They're plentiful this year, too. Mrs. Dorrance can have roses as well as flowers from the cutting beds for the party Wednesday night." He paused and then asked, "Begging your pardon, miss, but what sort of flowers do you plan to wear for the party?"

"I hadn't thought." After a moment I added, in a wry tone, "I'll wear a green dress." Green is about the only color that doesn't fight with sandy hair and a florid complexion.

"Good. I have just what you'll need. A small, pale green rose. Green Ice, it's called, and it's quite rare. I planted it last fall."

He moved ahead of me down the walk and then stopped. "There you are."

I looked at the buds of palest green. They would go well indeed with my darker green dress.

"Those buds should be opened just about enough by late Wednesday," he said. "I could make up a corsage for you. A few sprigs of lily-of-the-valley, and some fern—"

"Oh, thank you, Thorsen." Previous summers he had made corsages for me to wear on festive occasions. Each time they had looked as lovely as any that a swain—if I'd had a swain—might have sent me from a florist's shop.

He never offered to make a corsage for Amanda. True, there were always a number of young men telephoning her days ahead of a party at the Dorrance house, hoping that they would have the privilege of providing the flowers she would wear. But even if that had not been the case, I somehow felt, Thorsen would not have offered to fashion her corsage. He was the one man I knew who, for some strange reason, appeared not to like Amanda.

He said, "When I've made up your flowers I'll hand them in the back door to one of the maids. She can put it in the icebox until the party. Well, I'd best get to the greenhouse, and finish potting my chrysanthemums."

A few minutes later I went back into the house and climbed the stairs. I, too, should write some letters, I had decided, and might as well get them out of the way before lunch. I went into my room. It was a pleasant room, with blue-flowered wallpaper, handsome mahogany furniture, and wide windows that over-looked the rear lawn and the reflecting pool.

One of the housemaids, a middle-aged brunette named Edith West, was tucking the white crewel bedspread around the long bolster. "Good morning, miss. So Thorsen has been showing you his roses."

"Yes, including the new green rosebush. He offered

me flowers from it for Miss Amanda's birthday party Wednesday night."

"I don't wonder." Bending, she picked up a length of white thread from the oval blue-and-white braided rug. "He favors you," she said, straightening, "a lot more than he does—" She broke off, looking confused.

I said, smiling, "A lot more than he does Miss Lucy, or Miss Amanda? Yes, he seems to." Because I had come to feel, over the previous summers, that Edith was a friend as well as one of the Dorrance servants, I added, "It's a unique experience for me to have a man liking me better than Amanda."

"Because of her looks, you mean. Well, just the other day Thorsen was saying to me that good looks in a woman are a curse."

"If they are," I said wryly, "they are a curse most women would trade any number of blessings for."

"Well, miss, I guess it's because of his daughter that Thorsen feels that way. Not that Amy Thorsen looked anything like Amanda. But she too was a real beauty, with blue eyes and real golden hair."

"I didn't know he had a daughter."

"Well, he does. She was their only child, his and his wife's, I mean. The wife died, oh, maybe twelve years ago. I was new here then, and Miss Amanda and the twins were small children. A few months after his wife died, his daughter went away. I guess she was about seventeen then."

"Went away? Why?"

"Well, she went wrong, miss."

She looked at me from the corner of her eye, as if

gauging whether or not I understood the term. Thanks to my mother, I did. Perhaps because she had been raised in Germany rather than in England or America during the Victorian era, she did not feel that girls should remain "innocent"—that is, ignorant—of such matters until after marriage.

Evidently Edith saw that I understood because she said, "Amy Thorsen ran away with this married man. He'd been head clerk of that big grocery store in Southampton. After a while he deserted her, and a while after that she went off her head. They say she's still in a state hospital in Pennsylvania."

"Oh, the poor woman! And poor Thorsen!"

"Yes, it's a great pity. Well, I had best see to Miss Lucy's room now."

When she had left I reflected that with an only child who had "gone wrong," it was little wonder that Thorsen thought of comeliness as a curse. No wonder he looked with disfavor on Amanda, who was not only beautiful but had a willfulness that, almost surely, reminded him of his wanton child.

Was Lucy Dorrance good-looking enough to appear "cursed" in his eyes? Perhaps. Or perhaps he would not have liked her anyway. Few people seemed to. There was something very off-putting about Lucy Dorrance.

I sat down at the small mahogany desk in one corner of my bedroom and drew letter paper toward me. I wrote letters until the little watch pinned to my shirtwaist told me it was almost time for lunch.

Like breakfast, luncheon in the Dorrances' East Hampton house was served as a buffet, not in the big formal dining room but in a smaller room with French doors opening onto the south lawn. When I came into the room the twins were at the sideboard, spooning food onto their plates. Mr. Dorrance was already seated at one end of the mahogany table. He said, getting to his feet, "Good afternoon, Emma," and then sat down again.

Even in casual summer clothes—cream-colored flannel trousers, white shirt with a soft collar, dark blue flannel jacket—John Dorrance looked like what he was, a banker. Dark hair sprinkled with gray, cool blue eyes behind rimless glasses, clean-shaven face. And yet something about him—perhaps the largeness of his head or the squareness of his jaw or the near-burliness of his shoulders—always made me think of men of more physically active occupations. Military men, say, or even pugilists.

I joined the twins at the buffet. Lawrence turned and smiled at me. Lucy looked at me with remote hazel eyes and nodded. I did not mind. Long since I had accepted the fact that Lucy did not like me. Her feeling, I was sure, was not prompted by anything in my own personality. It was just that I was the best friend of her foster sister, the beautiful sister who was John Dorrance's favorite family member. I could understand her resentment and even sympathize with it. How galling to know that he gave first place in his affections to someone who was not even his own flesh and blood.

The twins turned away from the sideboard and carried their laden plates to the table. As I placed cold chicken slices and green salad on my own plate, I

21

reflected that a person judging by surface appearance would not have taken Lawrence and Lucy for brother and sister, let alone twins. He had gray eyes and fine, fair hair waving loosely back from a high forehead. She had hair as dark and thick as her father's once must have been, and a small-featured face set on a long neck. It was the sort of neck that is called swanlike, and it should have been beautiful, but was not. Perhaps it was a fraction of an inch too long. Anyway, its slender whiteness—she seldom went out into the sun—was faintly repellent.

In some ways, though, the twins were alike. They both were thin and inclined to be silent in company, although several times when 1 had come upon them unexpectedly in some room of the house or somewhere on the grounds, I had found them talking animatedly to each other. Neither of them cared for active sports. I don't imagine that their father minded Lucy's physical indolence. After all, she was considered delicate. But more than once I had heard him wax sarcastic about his son's record at Harley, the prep school he himself had attended. John Dorrance had been a member of the football and rugby teams, and captain of the ice hockey team. Lawrence had failed to win a place on any team.

One night only the week before, while we were having after-dinner coffee in the library, I had heard Mr. Dorrance say, with mock cheerfulness, "But it will be different when you go to Princeton in the fall, won't it, son? I'll be going over to Princeton every fall weekend to cheer you on when you're heading for that goal line with the football tucked under your arm."

Face dyed with painful-looking color, fingers tightening around the handle of his coffee cup, Lawrence had looked silently at his father.

Now, carrying my filled plate, I walked to the luncheon table and sat down. Mr. Dorrance asked, "Where's Amanda?"

"Writing letters, I think. I imagine she'll be down soon."

He nodded and then said, "Lucy wants me to bring her back a music box from Switzerland. What would you like, Emma?"

"Then you're going to Switzerland?"

"Yes. And to London and Paris and Florence and Rome. Probably I'll be gone most of the summer."

There was no need to ask if it was a business trip. I knew it must be. His bank, the largest in New York, had interests in half a dozen countries. Nor did I need to ask if Mrs. Dorrance would go with him. I knew she would not. They appeared together in public often enough—at the opera and charity events and a few private parties—to satisfy convention. But when at home they seemed almost to live in separate establishments. For days at a time Mrs. Dorrance kept to her own quarters, which were on the third floor of the townhouse and in the west wing out here, taking not only breakfast and lunch there but dinner also.

"Well, Emma, shall I bring you a music box too?"

"That would be lovely, Mr. Dorrance."

"And you, Larry? I don't imagine you want a music box. At least I hope you don't! And so what will it be?"

Lawrence's face had flushed, but his voice was even. "Anything you care to bring, sir."

"Now that's no answer. But wait a minute! I've got it. What's the name of that English poet whose book I found you reading the other day?"

"A. E. Housman, sir."

"That's right. I remember feeling relieved that it wasn't Oscar Wilde. Now is this Housman fellow still alive?"

Larry's flush had deepened. "I suppose so, sir. He started publishing only fifteen years ago."

"Good. I'll have some clerk in our London branch buy the fellow's books and then hunt him down and have him autograph them. How would you like that?"

Near-hatred in Lawrence's gray eyes. "That would be splendid, sir."

Amanda came into the room. I saw her father's face light up. "So there you are."

She kissed his cheek, filled her plate at the buffet, and then sat down beside me.

"It's settled, Amanda. I'm sailing for Europe next Saturday. What sort of present do you want me to bring back?"

"You'll be in Paris?"

"Yes. And London and Zurich and Florence and Rome."

"Then I'd like perfume from Paris. I'll write down the kind. And a gilt boudoir clock from Switzerland— something with cupids or doves or garlands in the frame—and three pairs of above-the-elbow white kid gloves from Florence."

He gave a delighted laugh. "You certainly know what you want, don't you?"

"Yes, Papa. I know what I want." She smiled at him and then turned to me. "Would you like to bicycle with me to the beach club this afternoon?"

There was a glint in her eye. I knew what it meant: If you come with me, don't pester me about canceling that invitation to Michael Doyle."

"Yes," I said, "I'd like to go bathing."

At the beach club we changed in two of the cabanas into our bathing costumes, which consisted of calf-length black dresses with sleeves that reached to just above the elbow. With them we wore black cotton stockings. For a while we paddled about in the not-too-deep water between the second and third lines of waves. Then, once more dressed in shirtwaists and skirts, we sat on the club veranda and drank lemonade.

At last I said, looking at my watch, "It's almost three. Hadn't we better start back?"

"You go on." She spoke with a promptness that made me realize that she had been waiting for me to suggest leaving. "I'd like to stay here for a while."

And so she had decided that she couldn't wait until Wednesday night. She must have phoned him at his boardinghouse and arranged a meeting. Would it be here at the club? Surely not. In no time word would reach the Dorrances that she had been seen on the club veranda with a strange man. And surely she didn't want her parents to know about Michael until Wednesday night, lest they forbid her to have him as a guest. No, she must have decided, better to face them with the *fait accompli* of his presence. Perhaps, with the giddy confidence of those in love, she had felt that once her

25

parents met Michael they would find him almost as irresistible as she did.

"Amanda—"

"Goodbye, Emma," she said, not smiling. "I'll see you at dinner."

I turned and left.

3

Thanks to a dynamo John Dorrance had installed the previous year in a shed attached to the carriage-house garage, the East Hampton house as well as the one in town had electricity. The night of Amanda's birthday party brilliant light beat down on the wide, flower-bedecked entrance hall.

As Amanda had told Michael Doyle, her mother liked formality. Thus there was a receiving line that night. As often happened, though, Mrs. Dorrance had felt the need of rest after dinner. Consequently Amanda had asked me to take her mother's place in the line for a while. From where I stood, flanked by Amanda and Lucy, I could see through the doorway into the lingering June dusk. Carriages and a few motor cars came up the U-shaped drive in a steady stream and discharged their passengers at the foot of the veranda steps. Because there were so many guests moving down the line I had little chance to talk to either of the Dorrance girls. But I was aware that Lucy, in ice-blue satin, greeted each newcomer at this party in honor of her foster sister by smiling a tight little smile and letting her hand lie limply in the guest's for a second or so. I was aware too that Amanda, radiant in rose taffeta, kept glancing away from whatever person she was greeting toward the new arrivals coming through the doorway.

On the other side of her stood her father. He loved parties, especially those attended by young people. Animation as well as an expanse of white shirt front made him look especially handsome that night. I had looked only briefly at Lawrence, standing at the foot of the line, but I knew that he appeared as stiff and withdrawn as his father appeared lively and outgoing.

At last Mrs. Dorrance, a still-handsome woman, as pale and thin as Lucy but with ash blond rather than dark hair, came down the stairs. I was free to join the dancers in the ballroom.

Even though she had consented to having a reception line, Amanda had insisted that there be no dance programs, so that the guests could follow the new fashion of "cutting in." And to insure that cutting in would be frequent, she had invited nearly twice as many men as girls. Almost as soon as I entered the ballroom a gangly youth whose name I could not recall asked me to dance. We had foxtrotted less than a minute to "Put Your Arms Around Me" when Dr. Carl Bauer, also tall but not in the least gangly, cut in. He was known as young Dr. Bauer to distinguish him from his father, Dr. Otto Bauer, but he did not look particularly young. In fact, a thickening waistline and heavy glasses, with gentle blue-gray eyes behind them, made him look at least half a dozen years older than his real age, which was thirty. From the first we had liked each other, perhaps because we were both of German ancestry. His father, like mine, still spoke with an accent.

"You are looking very fit tonight, Emma."

Not exactly a compliment to set a girl's heart to racing. But then, one of the things I liked about Carl Bauer was his ingenuousness.

"Thank you. Are you out here for a while?" Although his practice was in New York, during the summers he spent weekends and vacations at his father's East Hampton house.

"Yes. I will be here until the second week in July."

He said something else, but I did not catch its meaning. Dismayed, I was staring over his somewhat burly shoulder.

Even though this was her own party, and even though many of the invited guests were yet to arrive, Amanda had deserted the receiving line. She was dancing with Michael Doyle. They danced without speaking, just smiling into each other's eyes. Although I knew how displeased her mother and father, particularly her father, must be, I could not help but think that Amanda and the young Irishman appeared so very right together—both dark, both stunningly good-looking, and both surrounded by that almost visible aura that seems to shimmer around those newly in love.

Carl Bauer had whirled me around. He asked, "Who is that man dancing with Amanda?"

Before I could answer someone cut in. When my gaze again found Amanda she had a new partner, a blond youth who had been one of those flocking around her since her Junior Assembly days. Even though two newly arrived young women sat partnerless on chairs against the wall, Michael Doyle was not dancing. He stood with gaze following Amanda, obviously waiting to reclaim her. His behavior could be considered almost as unmannerly as Amanda's desertion of her own receiving line. But then, as Jane Austen remarked, a general uncivility is one of the first characteristics exhibited by those in love.

The five-piece orchestra on a platform at one end of the ballroom played on. "The Blue Danube" and "Daisy, Daisy," and "By the Light of the Silvery Moon." I danced twice more with Carl Bauer, once more with the gangly youth, and with several others. Most of the time when my gaze found Amanda she was dancing with Michael Doyle.

I became aware that the receiving line had broken up. Mrs. Dorrance must have gone up to bed, but the twins were in the ballroom. Lawrence, wearing a strained smile, danced with a plump girl in white. Lucy, not even bothering to smile, danced with Carl Bauer. In contrast to his bulky height, she looked like a thin, pale child.

Her father stood beside the long table at one side of the ballroom, a crystal punch cup in his hand and a fixed smile on his lips. Even at that distance I could tell, by his heightened color and by a glitter in his eyes, how very furious he was. He was letting his gaze wander over the crowd rather than focus on Amanda and Michael, dancing with that blissful, blind-to-the-rest-of-world look on their faces. But I felt sure that it was only unwillingness to risk creating a scene that kept him from ordering the stranger from his premises.

The next time I looked around he had gone. Perhaps he had felt that he could not control his rage any longer.

It must have been about eleven o'clock when Michael Doyle cut in on my partner of the moment. We moved across the floor for perhaps thirty seconds to the strains of "Artist's Life." Then he said, "Miss Hoffsteader, before someone cuts in—I mean, is there someplace we can go and talk for a few minutes."

We walked through a doorway at one end of the ballroom onto a glass-enclosed porch and then out onto the south lawn. The night was warm and the moonless sky bright with stars. We moved about fifty feet along a graveled path and then sat down on a marble bench.

He said, "What I wanted to talk to you about was—" and then stopped.

After a moment I said, "Don't tell me. Let me guess."

He threw me a startled look and then laughed. "I guess I'm pretty obvious."

"You both are."

He was silent for a moment. Finally he asked, "You don't like me, do you, Miss Hoffsteader?"

"How could I dislike you when I don't even know you? What I do dislike is anything that could cause a breach between Amanda and her family. The Dorrances are my friends. I don't like to see them made unhappy, especially Amanda."

"Perhaps you will call it conceit, but I think that by now she would be unhappy if we parted."

"Yes, for a short time." I paused. "You said 'by now.' I suppose that means that you've seen each other during the past few days."

"Three times. Miss Hoffsteader, won't you put in a good word for me with her parents? She tells me that they like and respect you." He paused and then said, "She would never want for anything. I would be able to support her well."

I wanted to say, so could a lot of other men, men of her own background. But I couldn't bring myself to say it.

"My father isn't nearly as rich as John Dorrance. But he has a good business, and it will grow. I'll help it to. I hadn't planned to stay with his business, but now I will."

"What had you intended to do?"

"I'd planned to paint pictures, at least for a year or two."

"Paint!"

"Yes, until I could be sure whether or not I was any good. I would have found some way to support myself while I was finding out."

"You've been to art school?"

"For a year I studied at the Manhattan Institute."

"What does your father—"

"He was puzzled and disappointed at first. But after a while he said that whatever I wanted to do was all right. My father—Well, I doubt that there is a finer man alive than my father. He also said that maybe it was in my blood to be some sort of artist. He says the story is that for a couple of hundred years the Doyles were bards."

"Bards? Those men who wandered about playing harps and reciting poetry they had written?"

"That's right. The Doyles were bards in the country around Loughglen."

"I never heard of it."

"It's a village in County Wicklow, on Ireland's eastern coast. I signed on a transatlantic freighter several summers ago, while I was still in college, and spent a week in Loughglen. That part of Ireland is so beautiful. Low stone walls, and sheep in fields so green they almost hurt your eyes. Lakes everywhere, and the ruins of castles on hilltops and of abbeys in the valleys. It's a haunted place, though."

"Haunted?"

"All Ireland is haunted, with the violence and pain and grief of the last four hundred years. I did some painting over there. I tried to get it on canvas. Not just the villages and fields and the faces of the Irish people, but that sadness . . ."

He went on speaking of Loughglen. His voice had taken on just the trace of an Irish lilt, as if he as well as his ancestors had been born in that vividly green country where peat smoke mingled with mist.

I think it must have been then that I, too, fell in love with Michael Terence Doyle. Oh, it was not a strong or serious love. How could it have been, with no hope to nourish it? But it was there in my heart, and it remained there for a long time.

"I don't have to paint, though," he said. "I'll gladly give it up, if I can have Amanda."

"You've asked her to marry you?"

"No, but I'm sure she knows I intend to. Do you think her parents will—accept me?"

I felt an obscure bitterness. "Look, Mr. Doyle, I am not Amanda's maiden aunt, even though I may act like it sometimes. I'm sure you have gathered what my advice is. If you and Amanda choose not to follow it . . .

Well, how can I be sure what her parents' reaction will be? I think I know, but I can't be sure. Now shall we go in?"

We moved back along the path through the starlight. Faintly I could hear the music of the orchestra. It was playing "Beautiful Dreamer."

4

As I moved along the hall toward the breakfast room the next morning, I could hear Mr. Dorrance's voice. He spoke so evenly that it was not until I had stepped through the doorway and heard him say, "—ever again set foot in this house," that I realized a family scene was taking place. Seated to his left, Amanda was glaring back at her father. On the opposite side of the table sat the twins. Both were smiling slightly, Larry with what obviously was nervous embarrassment, his sister with equally obvious pleasure.

I turned to leave. Mr. Dorrance said sharply, "No, Emma! I want you to hear this, too. Get yourself some breakfast and sit down."

Wanting to leave, but not knowing just how to do it, I walked over to the sideboard and helped myself to scrambled eggs and toast. When I'd sat down beside Amanda her father said, "That Doyle fellow will never be admitted to this house again. I have just told Amanda that, and I told the fellow himself earlier. I knew there was little likelihood he was anyone's house guest, and so this morning I telephoned the boardinghouses until I located him."

He went on, "I've also told Amanda that she is not to meet him outside this house. Now, have I made myself clear?"

"No, Papa." Anger, expanding her pupils, made her eyes look darker. "You haven't yet said what you'll do if I go on seeing Michael. What will you do? Disinherit me?"

"It might come to that."

"And I might not mind. Money isn't everything, you know."

"How could you know how important money is or isn't? You've always had plenty of it."

"Michael can have money, if he chooses. His father's business is successful, and—"

"If I decide to, I can fix it so that neither of the Doyles has any money."

"Oh, Papa! What are you going to do? Exile Michael and his father to Siberia? This isn't Russia, and you're not Czar Nicholas."

"Nevertheless, my smug little ignoramus, I am more powerful than you realize. Now I mean it, Amanda. I'm still going to Europe, because it's too late to change my plans. But if you see this Doyle fellow during my absence, even once— Well, I'll make you both wish you hadn't when I get back."

He threw down his napkin, shoved back his chair, and left the room.

Lucy said, into the silence, "He's only bluffing,

Amanda. He won't disinherit you, and there's nothing he can do to your friend Michael."

I looked at the small pale face with its little cat's smile. Plainly she was glad that Amanda had been unwise enough to fall in love with a young man of unacceptable background. And plainly she hoped that her sister would persist in her folly.

Probably Amanda realized that. Anyway, she made no reply but just sat there, crumbling a piece of breakfast roll with her fingers.

John Dorrance sailed for Europe three days later. I am almost certain that Amanda did not see Michael during those three days, nor for several days thereafter. She and I were together most of that time, bicycling to the beach, or driving to Southampton in the pony cart to go shopping, or playing Russian bank in what we called the tower room. It was in the third-floor turret at the southeast corner of the house, and it had been one of our favorite spots ever since I had started spending part of my summers with the Dorrances. I regret to say that the summer we were fourteen we sometimes dropped water-filled paper bags onto the head of one of the gardeners, a Chinese, who took care of the flower beds bordering a flagstoned terrace far below. We'd long since outgrown such mischief, but we still liked to play cards up there, or write in the diaries we kept locked in a table drawer, or just talk.

She did not mention Michael during the first days after her father left, nor did I. Perhaps, I thought, she had resolved to put him out of her life. In that case, the last thing I wanted to do was to remind her of him.

Mr. Dorrance had been gone five days when, for the third time since his departure, Mrs. Dorrance joined the rest of us for lunch. It was only when her husband was present, apparently, that she felt unable to leave her rooms for most of her meals. Looking at her face, calm between its two wings of ash blond hair, I often wondered if, before they had begun to treat each other like strangers, they had hurled bitter words back and forth, and if so, from what cause.

Toward the end of the meal Amanda said, "Mother, I'm afraid I'll have to go into town to see Dr. Ritter." Dr. Ritter, with offices on East Forty-second Street, was the Dorrances' dentist. "Last night one of my back teeth on the upper left side began to throb. And there's no one out here who can attend to it, not since Dr. Esterhazen retired."

"Perhaps it's a wisdom tooth," Mrs. Dorrance said, "although you're a little young for that sort of problem. Do you think that you can wait until Monday to go into New York? I'm sure the pharmacist here can give you something to make you comfortable. And I did promise to run one of the booths at the Childrens' Society benefit tomorrow—"

"But, Mother! You don't have to go into town with me. Emma can go. We'll spend several days, so that we can shop, and perhaps go to a matinee. And if you don't consider Emma enough of a chaperone, well, Mrs. Nesbitt is there."

The housekeeper, Mrs. Nesbitt, was the only servant who stayed in the Fifth Avenue house during the summer. The others either came out to the East Hampton house or were furloughed until the fall.

John Dorrance, I was sure, would never have allowed Amanda to spend several days in New York, chaperoned only by a girl her own age and by an upper servant. But Mrs. Dorrance said, "Very well. Go tomorrow if you like."

Her words did not surprise me. As I have said, I long had been aware that Mrs. Dorrance viewed her adopted daughter—that beautiful daughter so much preferred by her husband to either of the children his wife had borne—with a certain detachment, even coolness. Not that I ever heard Mrs. Dorrance speak harshly or even sharply to her adopted child, whereas she did sometimes reprimand Lucy for getting insufficient exercise, Larry for reading in a poor light, and both of them for lack of "sociability." It was only in Mrs. Dorrance's eyes that I read something that was almost dislike of Amanda.

Amanda never complained to me about her mother's attitude, but in little ways she showed that she was aware of it. For instance, although she called Mr. Dorrance "Papa," Mrs. Dorrance was "Mama" only to the twins.

Now Amanda said, "Thank you, Mother." Then, to me: "You would like to go to New York for a few days, wouldn't you?"

I was sure that Amanda had not told the truth, or at least not the whole truth, about her reasons for wanting to go to the city. Every instinct told me to steer clear of whatever trouble she might be inviting. I said, "New York in the summer isn't my idea of a pleasant place. If you don't mind, I'll stay out here."

Evidently Amanda feared that not even her mother would allow her to go into New York completely unaccompanied, because she said pleadingly, "Oh, Emma! The city isn't really hot, not yet."

Mrs. Dorrance said, "Don't try to force Emma to go. I'll go in with you next Monday. Surely you can wait until then."

"Mother! My tooth hurts! And nothing the pharmacist can give me will help for more than a little while."

I studied the lovely face. Was she really in pain? I could imagine her twenty-four hours from now, out here with no competent dentist within miles, holding her swollen jaw and moaning.

"All right, I'll go. It will give me a chance to get over to Brooklyn." I had not seen my parents for three weeks, and I missed them.

She beamed at me. "Thank you, Emma." She looked at the twins. Seated at the far end of the table, those strangely similar smiles on their faces, they had been talking in low tones to each other for the past few minutes.

Amanda said, "Is there anything I can get either of you in the city?"

Lucy's voice was bland. "Oh, I'm sure you'll be far too busy to shop for us. And anyway, I don't want anything. Do you, Larry?"

He shook his head.

Amanda gave her foster siblings a level look. "Very well," she said.

We caught the first train to New York the next morning. Our seats were in the parlor car. To people like the Dorrances, it would have been unthinkable for well-bred young women to ride unescorted in the coach, with no white-jacketed porter to protect them from the possible advances of strange men. Through the car's wide windows we watched the farmlands and villages of eastern and central Long Island give way to larger towns and then to the grimy outskirts of Queens.

When we reached New York, we followed a porter, laden with our valises, through the brand new splendors of Pennsylvania Station to the street. The driver of a horse-drawn cab helped the porter place our luggage atop the vehicle, and then drove us across town and up Fifth Avenue. The leaves of trees lining the wide street still retained some of the pale greenness of spring. Sunlight shone on the vehicles moving up and down the avenue. Each year for as long as I could remember the number of motor cars on the streets had increased. Now it seemed to me that not more than two-thirds of the vehicles were hansoms, carriages, or dray wagons. As for the horse-drawn Fifth Avenue coaches I remembered from my early childhood, they had been replaced entirely by motor omnibuses.

Amanda had telephoned Mrs. Nesbitt as well as Dr. Ritter before we left East Hampton. Consequently when we reached the Dorrance house the housekeeper, a stout, pleasant-faced woman in her fifties, opened the door to us before we reached the top of the steps. The hansom driver placed our valises on the black-and-white marble floor of the hall, accepted the fare and a tip from Amanda, and left. As we followed Mrs. Nesbitt toward the foot of the stairs, I could see through an open doorway to the drawing room, with its white-sheeted furniture looking ghostly in the dim light filtering through drawn blinds. On the second floor Amanda and I parted. I went into the room I always occupied when a guest in this house, a pleasant if rather noisy room overlooking the avenue, and Amanda walked back toward her own room with its view of the garden.

Mrs. Nesbitt served us a late luncheon in a small room off the library. Soon afterward Amanda left to keep her dental appointment, and I went for a walk, crossing from Fifth Avenue to Madison to look into shop windows. When I returned I found Amanda in the drawing room. She had not raised the shades which protected the magnificent rose and ivory Kerman from sun fading, but she had taken the dust sheet off the grand piano. She sat on the piano bench, picking out "Shine On, Harvest Moon" with one finger. She'd had nearly a year of piano instruction, but it had never, so to speak, taken. In fact, to her delight her piano teacher finally had told the Dorrances that even if they were willing to waste their money, he was not willing to waste any more time on such a thoroughly untalented pupil.

As I came into the room she turned to smile at me. "Mrs. Nesbitt said you'd gone for a walk."

"That's right."

"Did you enjoy it?"

"Yes. Now, how about you?"

"What do you mean, how about me?"

"Your tooth, of course. What did Dr. Ritter say?"

"Oh, that. He doesn't want to pull it unless he has to. He put something on my gum to keep down inflammation. I'm to see him again next Friday."

That meant staying a week in New York. I studied her

face, with its violet eyes that looked so candidly into mine. Had Dr. Ritter really requested that she stay that long? Had she, in fact, even seen him? I could not find out without telephoning him or going to his office, and I had no intention of doing that. I turned and climbed the stairs to my room to take off my hat.

5

In midmorning the next day I went over to Brooklyn. After that Fifth Avenue mansion with its crystal chandeliers and rich carpets, and after that East Hampton house filled with chintz and wicker furniture and sunlight, the décor of my parents' narrow brownstone seemed dull and heavy. Dark woodwork, thick draperies of bottle-green velvet at the long windows, and on the walls, in heavy gilt frames, time-dimmed oils from Germany, mostly of woodland scenes, or of plump burghers drinking in inns or gathered with their families around food-laden tables. But I loved this house, the only home I'd ever known, and I loved the two gentle people in it. I had a sense of being wrapped in safety and peacefulness as soon as I walked in the front door.

Since it was Sunday, dinner was served at one. My parents and I sat at the round dining room table beneath the many-bracketed gaslight chandelier with its dark red, tulip-shaped globes. My father, with his grizzled mustache and with a napkin tucked into his collar, looked not unlike a figure in one of those paintings of domestic scenes on the walls. My mother wore her hair just as she had in a tintype of her as a bride. The blond braids around her head had lots of gray now, but her plump face still held much of the freshness of a young girl.

When the three of us were alone, we usually spoke German. My father said, helping himself to more sauerbraten, "It must feel strange, being in that big house with no one else there except Amanda and the housekeeper."

"It does, rather."

"I wonder that Mr. Dorrance allowed it. He impressed me as being strict in such matters. Overstrict, I would say. But then," he added, beaming at me, "maybe Mama and I would be the same if we didn't have such a sensible, levelheaded daughter."

"Thank you, Papa. But as I told Mama when I came in, Mr. Dorrance isn't here. He sailed for Europe."

"Just the same," my mother said, "I wonder that Mrs. Dorrance permitted it. Surely she doesn't want to displease her husband."

For several moments I remained silent. My parents were proud that their daughter, because of her friendship with Amanda Dorrance, had been invited to the Junior Assemblies, and later on to parties in some of New York's most exclusive houses. I did not want to tell them of the undercurrents I'd been aware of in both the Fifth Avenue house and the one in East Hampton. The estrangement between John and Clara Dorrance. Mr. Dorrance's cruel jibes at his withdrawn, unathletic son. The sly, malicious smile that Lucy so often directed at her beautiful foster sister. The way the twins seemed to huddle together, excluding everyone from their mur-mured confidences. And the odd detachment with which Clara Dorrance seemed to regard all her children, especially Amanda.

At last I said, "Perhaps Mrs. Dorrance doesn't have the energy for much discipline, Mama. She's been in delicate health as long as I've known her."

"Ach, poor woman. I heard she never got her strength back after her twins were born. It was the same with poor Mrs. Weiler. Papa, you remember the Weilers. They used to run the shoe repair shop until they lost it."

With the conversation turned to the unfortunate Weilers, I could relax.

In late afternoon I said goodbye to my parents and took the subway, opened only two years before, which ran beneath the East River to Grand Central Station. From there I rode up Fifth Avenue in one of the new motor coaches. I had left the coach at the Sixty-second Street stop and was walking back a half block through the near-sunset light when I saw the hansom cab standing before the Dorrance house. I quickened my pace. The front door opened. The housekeeper came down the steps, valise in hand, and crossed the sidewalk.

"Mrs. Nesbitt!"

She turned a pleased, excited face to me. "Oh! Hello, Miss Hoffsteader."

"You are going somewhere?"

"Yes! To Baltimore, to see my grandson. Just think! He's eight months old, and I have never seen him." The coachman had descended from the box. She handed him her valise.

I asked, "Does Mrs. Dorrance know—"

"That I'm going? Oh, yes. Miss Amanda arranged it, the darling. Without even telling me—she wanted it to be a surprise—she telephoned her mother this morning. Mrs. Dorrance said that since you were here it would be all right for me to spend a few days with my daughter and her husband and my grandson."

Had Mrs. Dorrance said that? I very much doubted it. No matter how indifferent she might be to her foster daughter, she would not want people to know that she had let Amanda stay unchaperoned, and accompanied only by me, in the townhouse. In fact, I doubted that Amanda had even telephoned her mother about Mrs. Nesbitt and her grandson. But it was scarcely my place to suggest to the housekeeper that Amanda had lied to her.

The hansom driver had placed the valise on the cab's roof and opened the door for his passenger. She said, "Goodbye, Miss Hoffsteader."

"Goodbye, Mrs. Nesbitt. Have a pleasant time." I went up the steps, hearing the clop of hooves as the cab pulled away from the curb.

I did not need to ring. In her excitement, Mrs. Nesbitt had left the door unlocked. Standing in the marble-floored hall I called, "Amanda?"

No answer. After a few seconds I climbed the stairs, walked past my room, and went on down the hall to Amanda's door. I knocked. "Come in," she called.

I found her standing in a pink muslin dress before a pier glass mirror, shaking out the flounces of her skirt. My nerves tightened when I saw the excited look on her face.

I said, "I just said goodbye to Mrs. Nesbitt."

"Then she's left? Oh, I suppose she must have. She planned to catch a six-fifteen train." Leaning close to the mirror, she smoothed one eyebrow with a fingertip.

"Amanda, did you ask your mother's permission to tell Mrs. Nesbitt she could go?"

She turned to face me. "All right, I didn't. Mother would never have let her go." Indignation came into her voice. "I think Mother and Papa should be ashamed of themselves. That poor, poor woman, so terribly eager all these months to see her grandson."

Yes, so eager that, apparently, she had not asked herself if it was not strange, under the circumstances, that her employer should be willing to let her go. Nor had she stopped to wonder, apparently, whether or not Miss Amanda might have reasons of her own to want her to go.

Then I told myself not to leap to conclusions. It could be that Amanda had acted only out of sympathy for the older woman. As I very well knew, Amanda was in many ways a generous and warm-hearted girl.

"Mrs. Nesbitt left us chicken salad for tonight," she said. "After that we'll take turns cooking. It will be fun, Emma."

"I'll go take off my hat," I said, and left her.

I had nearly reached my room when I heard the doorbell ring. I went down the stairs and opened the door. In white flannels and blue blazer, straw hat in his hand, dark curly hair bronzed by sunset light, Michael Doyle stood on the doorstep.

Despite my resolution of a few minutes before to give Amanda the benefit of the doubt, I had expected

Michael to arrive soon after Mrs. Nesbitt's departure. Perhaps I had expected it ever since Amanda developed her toothache.

He was smiling. "Well, Miss Hoffsteader, aren't you going to ask me in?"

"It is not my house," I said coldly. Nevertheless, I opened the door wider. When he stood in the hall I asked, "Did you know that the housekeeper would not be here?"

"Yes."

"I'll just bet you did."

"May I?" He laid his hat on the hall table and then turned and took both my hands. A kind of tingling warmth traveled up my arms. "Please, Emma! It's all right if I call you Emma, isn't it? You understand. I know you do. You're young too. Amanda and I are in love. If we could see each other openly— But that's been forbidden. And we were afraid that if the housekeeper knew I was here, she'd feel obliged to let the Dorrances know."

Muffled footsteps sounded over the carpeting in the hall above. Michael released my hands, for which I was glad. Amanda was coming down—almost floating down—the stairs in her pink dress. I shot a glance at Michael. The look on his upturned face as he watched her seemed to light up the whole hall, now filled with deepening shadows.

At the foot of the stairs she said softly, "Hello, Michael." Then she turned to me, mingled guilt and triumph in the lovely violet eyes. Once again she had presented me with the *fait accompli*. "Don't scold, Emma. Please don't scold."

49

In my resentment I spoke the phrase I had used during my conversation with Michael the night of her birthday party. "Why should I scold? I'm not your maiden aunt." I climbed the stairs.

The three of us had supper that night in the little room off the library. To accompany the chicken salad and tomato aspic and fresh strawberries, Amanda had brought up a bottle of Riesling from the cellar. Perhaps it was the wine. Or perhaps the look in their two faces, and the aura of exhilaration around them, extended itself to me. Whatever the reason, I found myself enjoying the meal, and laughing at the jokes Michael told in an Irish brogue. After supper the three of us did a sketchy washing-up in the kitchen and then went to the drawing room.

"Michael, roll up one or two of those rugs," Amanda said. Then, to me: "You'll play, won't you, Emma?"

Since my first lessons when I was eight, I had enjoyed the piano. I played "Over the Waves," and "Skater's Waltz," and "Juanita," and Amanda's favorite, "Put Your Arms Around Me, Honey." I tried to subdue both my disapproval and that wistful, nagging envy in my heart. I told myself to concentrate upon my pleasure in the music, and to feel nothing but admiration for the way Michael and Amanda appeared as they danced, both so almost incredibly good-looking, both with that dazed and yet acutely alive look in their eyes.

At last Michael said, "Poor Emma! She's been playing long enough. Didn't I see a phonograph in that parlor across the hall?"

He went to the parlor and then returned, weighted down with the phonograph and its flaring horn. As he set the machine down on a table I got to my feet. If only for politeness sake, he would now ask me to dance. And I felt that the less Michael touched me the better.

"Goodnight," I said. "I'm a little tired, what with my trip to Brooklyn and all." Despite their polite protests, I went upstairs to bed.

For a while I heard the phonograph playing "Shine On, Harvest Moon," and "Yellow Rose of Texas," and "I Love You Truly." Then a long silence. Then, coming up the stairs, passing my room, and continuing down the hall toward Amanda's room, two pairs of footsteps. A door softly opened and closed.

That, too, did not surprise me. It shocked and dismayed me, yes, but it did not surprise me. I think that somewhere deep in my mind I had known, ever since John Dorrance had made his threats concerning Michael Doyle, that sooner or later headstrong Amanda would come to this moment.

Nor did I reproach myself with the thought that if I had stayed down in the drawing room tonight, Michael would have gone docilely out the front door. Oh, he might have gone, all right, but only after they had arranged that later on she would creep down the stairs and let him back in.

I did not hear him leave the house. By that time I had, at long last, fallen asleep.

6

When I came downstairs the next morning I saw no sign of Amanda. In the kitchen I prepared a sketchy breakfast of tea and toast and ate it at the kitchen table. Then, needing to escape this silent house, I went upstairs for my hat. Because the day seemed cooler than the one before, I also put on my spring coat of brown merino.

I was halfway down the stairs when I heard running footsteps. I halted and turned. Wearing a turquoise kimona, her face still flushed with sleep in its frame of disordered curls, Amanda stood on the stair landing. She looked at me for a long moment and then asked, "Where are you going?"

"For a walk."

"Wait! I'll come with you."

Before I could answer she turned and hurried back toward her room. I descended the rest of the stairs and then sat down in a high-backed, Spanish-style chair in the hall, wishing I had been able to make my escape before she left her room.

Sooner than I expected she came down the stairs,

dressed for the street in a dark blue alpaca jacket and skirt trimmed with black braid. Her hat, also of dark blue, was one of the newly fashionable toques.

"Aren't you going to have breakfast?" I had tried to speak naturally, but there was a coldness in my voice.

"Later. I'd rather walk first."

We went out into the cool, overcast day. Traffic moved along the avenue with Monday morning briskness. We had crossed the first intersection before she finally spoke. "So you know."

"Yes."

We walked on in silence. At Sixty-eighth Street I crossed the avenue to the park, and she crossed with me. It was not until we were moving up the mall between the twin lines of mostly vacant benches that she spoke again. She said, in a tone of forced lightness, "So you know I'm a fallen woman."

I glanced from the corner of my eye at my beautiful friend, looking every inch the *jeune fille bien élevée* in her smart but demure spring clothes. How strange to think that she was indeed a fallen woman. Until now I had somehow assumed that girls of Amanda's class didn't fall. Oh, perhaps in decadent old Europe they did. But not in America. In this country, I had felt, women who fell were housemaids, or factory girls, or girls like that poor daughter of Thorsen's.

When I did not answer she said, "Could we sit down for a moment? My feet hurt. I don't know what I was thinking of, but I put on the shoes I haven't worn since I bought them in Southampton last week."

We sat down on a bench. Instantly pigeons settled on the walk at our feet, regarding us with round, greedy eyes. When they realized we had nothing to give them they moved away, heads bobbing. Amanda said, "Do you plan to tell my parents?"

"You know better than that."

She turned to me with contrition in her face. "I'm sorry. Of course I know you wouldn't." She paused. "Although maybe it would be just as well if Papa did find out. Now that I'm what people call ruined, he'd have to let me marry Michael."

I was not so sure of that.

She went on, "I know what you think of me, Emma. But it wouldn't have happened if Papa had allowed me to see Michael, allowed us to have a courtship, and engagement, and marriage. But he would never grant us that. And so last night—Oh, Emma! I love Michael so much. Can't you understand how it happened?"

In a way I could. At least I could understand, only too well, how she might love Michael. And even though I tended to be much more conservative than Amanda—like my idol, Jane Austen, I believed that to break society's rules almost always brought unhappiness—even so, I could see how she would rebel against the idea that Michael, merely because of his background, was a man she should not marry.

But that was the summer of 1910, remember. What's more, I was the descendant of a long line of pious Lutherans. I could not, I simply could not, tell her that I condoned what she had done.

When I remained silent, she said, "Well, what do you intend to do? Go home to Brooklyn?"

"Yes." What else could I do, if Amanda intended to continue entertaining her lover in her bedroom?

"Please, Emma! Please don't desert me. I won't let him . . . stay at the house again. I won't even let him come there, if you think that best." It was only later that I realized that she had not promised to meet him elsewhere. "I *need* you, Emma. I'm so very much alone."

That was true, I realized. Her mother was aloof to the point of indifference. The twins seemed to have no need to receive her affection or to give her theirs. And now she and her father were estranged.

"Please, Emma. Please stay. I need you to help me with something, something I've wanted to do for a long time."

I thought of how kind she had been to me, a plain, rather shy day pupil who otherwise might have had no real friends at Miss Bradley's. I thought of how she had opened up a whole world to me—a world where graceful people moved from tennis court to bridle path to sailing yacht—which otherwise I probably never would have known.

And I felt more than gratitude. I was fond of her, surely as fond as I would have been of a sister if I'd had one.

Nevertheless, I felt wary. "What is it you want me to help you with?"

She was silent for a moment and then burst out, "I think my parents lied to me. I think they do know who my real mother was, and perhaps my father too. And *I* want to know.

"Think how you'd feel, Emma, if you didn't have your parents. I know how much you love them. What if you'd never even known them? What if instead you'd had—"

She broke off, but I knew what she had meant. For a

moment I thought of what it would be like to have never known my warm-hearted parents, to have been raised instead by a withdrawn, always ailing woman like Clara Dorrance and man like John Dorrance, a man frequently absent, and, when present, overindulgent in some ways and tyrannical in others.

But I felt that the chances were small indeed that Amanda's natural parents, even if she did find them, would turn out to be like my parents.

I said, "Please, please, Amanda. Leave well enough alone." When she did not answer, but instead just gazed obstinately down at the tip of one shiny new shoe, I went on, "And anyway, how do you plan to try to find out? If that lawyer who handled the adoption is dead— And even if he isn't, even if they lied to you about that, how can you find him? Did your parents ever mention his name?"

"No." She made an impatient gesture. "But that doesn't matter."

"What do you mean, it doesn't matter?"

"I'm going to hire a private detective. I bought a copy of the *Clarion-Telegraph* yesterday." The *Clarion-Telegraph,* devoted to divorce cases and to frenzied editorials about the need for a Great White Hope to defeat the Negro boxing champion Jack Johnson, was not the sort of newspaper respectable people allowed into their homes. "This detective, Paul Marsden, had an advertisement in it. It said, 'Do you need to know the truth about your spouse? Do you need to trace someone, whether living or dead? See Paul Marsden.'"

"Oh, Amanda. No telling what sort of man—"

"He has a telephone," she went on, as if I hadn't

spoken. "The number was printed in the advertisement. When we get back to the house I'll call him. If there's a record somewhere about my real mother, it might take you and me weeks to find it. But a detective should know just where to search."

I looked at her flushed, determined face. Why this overwhelming urge to find her real mother? Was she hoping that her mother would not only welcome her, but give loving approval to Michael as well, an approval the Dorrances would never grant her?

"Please, Emma. Please stay."

More than ever I wanted to go to the Fifth Avenue house, pack my bag, and start out for the narrow old brownstone in Brooklyn, a house only across the river, and yet a world away from my reckless friend and whatever disasters her willfulness might lead her to. But that was just it. She was my friend. And my presence, at least to a certain extent, might temper both her folly and its consequences.

I stood up, scattering a new group of pigeons who had gathered in hope of a handout. "All right. Let's go back to the house."

7

Paul Marsden called on us the next morning. Never having met a private detective, I had not known what to expect. Because of the Conan Doyle illustrations, I suppose I would not have been surprised if he had turned out to be hawk-nosed gentleman in a cloak and a deerstalker cap. Instead he was a small, rather furtive-looking man in brown shoes, a navy blue suit, and a collar that should have been sent to the laundry several days before.

The three of us sat in the smaller of the two parlors, on straight chairs from which we had removed the dust covers. I saw his brown eyes dart quick glances at the crystal chandelier and across the hall to the grand piano and oriental rugs in the drawing room. I had the feeling that he was estimating, not only the cost of the mansion and its furnishings, but also how much he could extract from the two ignorant young females who had summoned him.

When we returned to the house from the park the day before, I had urged Amanda to delay telephoning him. "Before you go to the expense of hiring a detective," I said, "why don't we go down to City Hall? Probably someone there can tell us where to find such a record, if it exists."

"No! I don't want to take a chance that word of what I'm doing will get to Mother or Papa. And I don't care how much it costs, as long as I can find out quickly. I'm going to go downtown this afternoon and sell my cameo pin with the seed pearls. That way I'll be sure to have enough to pay him."

Now, as she told him what she wanted to know, I saw a flash of amusement, quickly veiled, in his eyes. It convinced me that he felt that the record of Amanda's adoption not only existed, but probably would be ridiculously easy to find.

He scribbled down the information she gave him— the year of her birth, the name of her adoptive parents—in a notebook with a worn black leather binding. Then he said, after tapping a yellow pencil against his teeth, "Nineteen years ago. It'll take some digging to find the record, if there is one. Now do you want me to try to locate your mother too, your natural mother, I mean?"

Amanda nodded, her face tense.

"Well, I can't guarantee results, you understand, but I'll do my best." He paused. "My fee will be sixty dollars. Thirty dollars now and the other thirty when I report back to you whatever I've found out."

Sixty dollars! Why, that was as much as my father's highest salaried employee made in a whole month. But even though Amanda's allowance was only fifteen dollars a month, she did not seem fazed by the size of the fee. She reached into the deep pocket of her skirt and brought out a change purse. From the bills inside she selected three tens and handed them to him. I had the impression that he wished he had asked for more.

"Thank you, Miss Dorrance," he said, and got to his feet. "I'll come back as soon as I have some information."

We did not hear from him during the next two days. Both those days Amanda left the house in the late afternoon, once ostensibly to have tea at the Waldorf with a former governess, and once to meet a friend named Audrey for shopping. ("You don't know her, Emma. I met her at dancing school when I was ten.") Both times she was already dressed for the street when she told me she was leaving, thus forestalling any offer to come with her. And both times she did not return until almost dark.

I had resolved not to spy on her and Michael, or to make any further efforts to keep them apart. But I did succumb, late on the second afternoon, to the temptation to look in the telephone book. It was a thin book in those days. Only a small percentage of New Yorkers had private telephones. Most small businesses got along without them too.

There was a business listing for Matthew Thomas Doyle Enterprises, in the Wall Street district, and a residential listing under the same name on East Twenty-third Street. And there was a listing for Michael T. Doyle at an address on Central Park South, only a few blocks from the Dorrance house. I wondered if Michael's apartment had a window overlooking the park. Feeling dismay and anxiety and—yes—envy, I thought of them standing by such a window, exchanging one last kiss before she walked home through the fading light.

She came in shortly before eight, wearing a dreamy look that never could have been the result of a shopping trip with an old friend. I asked no questions when, over the supper table, she told me that she and Audrey had spent "hours" window-shopping after Lord and Taylor's closed.

We were at breakfast the next morning when the telephone out in the hall rang. She went to answer it and then came back, excitement in her face, to tell me that it had been Paul Marsden. He had the information she wanted, and would bring it to her at one that afternoon.

Why he did not delay calling her for several more days, so as to give the impression that the task was indeed difficult, I don't know. Perhaps he was too impatient to collect the other half of his fee. Perhaps also he felt that with two naive creatures like us he did not have to be clever.

That afternoon, again seated in the small parlor, he said, "Well, it took some digging. I had to stop everything else so as to find out what you want to know. But I finally got it. On June 18, 1891, a Rose Shannon surrendered a five-day-old female infant for adoption by John and Clara Dorrance."

Amanda leaned forward. "This Rose Shannon," she asked tautly, "is she—"

"Yes, she's alive. I got her address, and believe me, that did take digging. Here it is. She's lived there for ten years." From the worn notebook he ripped out a page and handed it to her.

Face flushed and excited, she read aloud, "'Mrs. Rose

Shannon, Five twenty West Eighteenth Street.' Are you sure this is right? I mean how did you find this address? Is she in the telephone book?"

He laughed. "On that block? Not that it's a slum, you understand, but it doesn't run to private telephones. As for how I found out . . . Well, every profession has its secrets, Miss Dorrance, and that's one of mine."

Although I felt sure that he had found the record of Amanda's adoption in some archive open to anyone, I was impressed by his tracking down her natural mother so quickly. Even though a reasonably intelligent girl, I had grown up in ignorance of many practical, everyday matters. Quite some time passed before I learned that there was such a thing as a city directory, and that it would have taken him only seconds to look up Rose Shannon's name in it.

Amanda said, "You've written down Mrs. Rose Shannon. Does that mean that she was married when—when—"

"All it means, young lady, is that I copied down the name I found on her mailbox. Whether she's married now, or ever was, I don't know. Of course I could find out a lot more about her, but that would cost you extra."

"No. We'll go see her."

Today she had laid her purse on a small table near her chair. She took three ten-dollar bills from it and held them out to him. "And five more for expenses," he said, as he pocketed the money. "I told you it would be sixty plus expenses, remember."

He had told her no such thing, and I knew from the way her eyes flashed that she knew he had not. Then, with an almost imperceptible shrug, she handed him an additional five dollars.

We both accompanied him to the front door. When she had closed it behind him she turned to me, triumph in her face. "Rose Shannon! It sounds Irish, doesn't it? Remember that day on the beach when I said how ridiculous it was for Papa to object to Michael's being Irish? I said that my own mother might have been Irish."

"I remember."

"You'll come with me, won't you, Emma, when I go to see her?"

Having come this far with her, I could not turn back. "Yes, I'll go with you."

8

The next afternoon a hansom cab took us to Rose
Shannon's address. While Amanda was paying the fare,
I saw the driver eyeing the building and wondering,
obviously, why two well-dressed young women should
have come here. As the detective had said, the place was
not actually a slum. There were no broken, patched-
over windows. No ragged children played on the front
steps. But the six-story building, with a red brick façade
that lacked all ornamentation, looked cheap and
depressing. I guessed that it housed what were called
railroad flats, with rooms strung out in a line like the
cars of a train.

The double door with its upper panes of smeared
glass was unlocked. In the small foyer we looked at the
row of glass-fronted mail boxes recessed into one wall.
Mrs. Rose Shannon, we saw, lived in flat 3-C. We
climbed a narrow stair with a heavily-varnished hand-
rail. There was a smell of cooking cabbage, and the
sound of someone's phonograph playing "Take Me Out
to the Ballgame." Since even my pulse had quickened, I
could imagine how tense Amanda must be.

At the door of 3-C Amanda hesitated, and then knocked. After a moment the door opened. The light—gaslight—was behind the woman who stood there, and so at first I had only an impression of disordered dark hair and some kind of loose garment.

She said, "Yes?" I became aware of the odor of alcohol.

Amanda asked, in a tight voice, "Are you Mrs. Rose Shannon?"

"That's right."

"I'm—I'm Amanda Dorrance."

The woman stiffened. Several moments passed. Then she said, "So after all this time, the Dorrances told you. Well, you'd better come in."

We stepped over the threshold. Then I saw why, at midafternoon of a sunny day, the gas jet on the wall had been lighted. The room's one window faced the wall of another tenement only about three feet away. Without artificial light, the place would have been dark indeed.

Amanda said in a constricted voice, "This is my friend, Emma Hoffsteader."

"Pleased to meet you, Miss Hoffsteader."

I could see her clearly now. She wore a yellow, slightly soiled kimona. Her dark curly hair had little sheen and there were puffs beneath her eyes—blue eyes, not violet. And yet there could be no doubt that she was Amanda's mother. In fact, at one time she must have been almost as beautiful as her daughter.

She said, "Well, sit down," and waved vaguely at a small sofa upholstered in worn, dark red plush. Amanda and I sat down side by side. Rose Shannon sat facing us in a rocker of dark wood. I realized now that I had been right in thinking this was a building of railroad flats. Over her shoulder I could see, beyond the doorway into the next room, a stove and a sink. The room beyond the kitchen apparently was a bedroom. I could see what appeared to be a chest of drawers. Although I did not look at Amanda, I knew the shrinking dismay she must feel at sight of this ugly little room with its garish chromo of a gypsy dancing girl on the wall, and its gas heater in a fake fireplace with a pink-skirted kewpie doll on the mantel. And of course she must be distressed most of all by Rose Shannon herself.

Amanda said, "Are you—are you really my mother?"

I saw a mixture of emotions in the puffy but still attractive face—embarrassment and wry regret and a kind of vague tenderness. "Yes, honey, I am. I guess a person would only have to look at the two of us to know that. But I don't see why the Dorrances told you. They've been supporting me all these years because I promised to keep quiet and never even try to see you."

"They—they picked out this place for you . . . ?"

"Oh, lord no, honey. They've never even seen this place, or the two other places I've lived in since you were born. They just send me fifty dollars a month. They don't care what I do with it."

Fifty dollars a month was a respectable sum. Surely she could have afforded better surroundings. Then, catching another whiff of whatever it was she had been drinking, I realized that part of that monthly stipend must be used to buy liquor.

Amanda said, "My parents didn't tell me about you, and they don't know that I am here. I—I hired a detective to find out who my mother was, and where she was."

"I see. Well, I wish you hadn't done it, honey. I'll bet your friend here said you shouldn't." She smiled at me. "Didn't you?"

I said, hesitantly, "Well, as a matter of fact—"

"I just knew you did. I can tell you're the sensible type." She looked at Amanda and then said gently, "It's not that I'm not pleased and proud to see you. What woman wouldn't be? I already knew you were beautiful. I saw your picture in the paper when you had your deb—deb—that party your folks gave you last winter. But of course it's a hundred times better to see you face to face. You shouldn't have come here, though, for your own sake. I know what you must be thinking about this place, and about—about . . ." She broke off.

Amanda remained silent for several seconds. From the corner of my eye I saw her clasped hands tighten in her lap. Finally she said, "Why, I don't think anything, except that you're—nice, and that I'm glad we look so much alike." Then, swiftly: "Tell me about my father. Were you—were you—"

"No, honey, I wasn't married. Do you think if I had been I'd have given you up? Rose Shannon is the name I've had all my life. I just tacked on the Mrs."

"Who was he?"

Rose Shannon looked away. "I'm not going to answer that."

"Why not? Why not?"

The woman returned her gaze to Amanda. She said, with that exaggerated air of candor some people assume when they are lying, "All right, if you have to know. His name was Earl Findley, and he's been dead for, oh, fifteen years now. He died in prison. That's why I didn't want you to know."

"Why was he in prison?" To my surprise, Amanda did not seem distressed by Rose's words.

"He was down on his luck and riding the rails, see. This railroad detective started beating him up. Earl got hold of the club and hit the cop over the head and it killed him. Earl wasn't bad. Just unlucky."

For several seconds there was no sound in the room except the faint hiss of the gas jet. Then Amanda said in a quiet voice, "I think you knew an Earl Findley who died in prison, but I don't think he was my father. Why are you trying to hide the truth from me?" When Rose Shannon did not answer, Amanda went on, "It's because my adoptive father and my real father are the same, isn't it? A—a kind of instinct has been telling me that for several years now."

The look on Rose Shannon's face was confirmation enough.

I wondered why I myself had not guessed the truth before this. As long as I had known the Dorrances I had been aware of John Dorrance's preference for Amanda over the twins. Moreover, although Amanda closely resembled Rose Shannon, she had a certain firmness of jaw that could remind one of John Dorrance's handsome face.

Amanda said, with a stubborn persistence that also reminded me of John Dorrance, "He is my father, isn't he?"

Rose Shannon's hands—long-fingered, sensitive hands that she should not have weighted with cheap rings—made a resigned gesture. "All right. But don't let Mrs. Dorrance know. Your father went to a lot of trouble to keep his wife from knowing that the baby they were going to adopt was his."

"I won't tell her." Then, after a pause: "How did you and my father—"

"We met while I was dancing at the Haymarket."

Even well brought-up girls had heard of the Haymarket, a combined café, dance hall, and variety theater which, until the reformers closed it down, had flourished on a corner not far from where the three of us now sat. I could remember how, when I was a child, the pastor of our Lutheran church had preached thunderous sermons against "Satan's Circus," which was what the whole district around the Haymarket was called. He also denounced the men, "some of them the most prominent and respected in this great city," who spent money there.

Among those prominent and respected men, apparently, had been John Dorrance.

Rose Shannon, gaze lowered, had begun to lay pleats in the yellow kimona and smooth them down over her knee. "John was already married, of course. He had been for several years. But—and I don't know how to say this except straight out—he had an eye for the ladies. Two other girls at the Haymarket had been his lady friends before he met me."

I threw a sidewise glance at Amanda. Her face had paled, but otherwise she appeared calm.

"When I told him I was going to have a baby, he said he and his wife would adopt it. The Dorrances didn't have any children, you know, not then. He fixed everything up with this lawyer. The lawyer told Mrs. Dorrance that he knew this girl who was in the family way." Color came into her face. "He didn't tell Mrs. Dorrance about the Haymarket, of course. He said that this girl was of a poor but nice family, and so was the boy who had gotten her into trouble. Mrs. Dorrance liked the sound of that. She agreed to take the lawyer's word for it, and not make him tell who the girl was."

She went on telling how, soon after Mrs. Dorrance had agreed to the adoption, she had found that she herself was pregnant. "Just the same, Mrs. Dorrance agreed to go through with the adoption. She'd already had a couple of miscarriages. I guess she was afraid she might have another one."

Rose Shannon had stopped pleating the skirt of her kimona. She smoothed out the material and said, in a flat voice, "You were born in a small hospital in Queens. The lawyer had told the hospital that you were to be taken from me right away. I figured that was best, too. Until today, I've seen you only a couple of times since, and then by accident. One day when you were seven I was on a Fifth Avenue coach passing the Dorrance house. A nursemaid and three kids came down the steps. I knew which one of the two girls was you, because you looked just like an old tintype I have of me around that age. And of course I knew that the boy and the other girl must be Mrs. Dorrance's twins. It had been in the paper when they were born. A couple of years later I saw you and your father and the twins in Central Park one Sunday. John didn't see me."

Amanda asked, in a strained voice, "Then you're not in touch with him at all?"

"No. Somebody in his office sends fifty a month—in cash, not a check—to a post-office box I have. But I never hear from John directly. Amanda, are you going to tell your father about coming here today?"

"I don't know. I couldn't tell him right away even if I wanted to. He's gone to Europe. Probably he'll be gone all summer."

"Even if you do tell him, be sure not to tell Mrs. Dorrance. There wouldn't be any point in hurting her, not when she's gone all this time without knowing the truth."

But had she, I wondered, been ignorant of the truth? Perhaps she too, long ago, had hired a detective to find out about the parentage of her adopted child. Perhaps she hadn't needed a detective. Perhaps, like Amanda, she had guessed the truth instinctively. She might even have challenged her husband with it. Now less than ever I wondered at her estrangement from both her husband and her adopted daughter.

Amanda said, "Of course I won't tell my moth— of course I won't let her know I've found out. What would be the point?" After a moment she added, "Could you tell me a little more? About my grandparents, I mean, and where you grew up, and so on?"

She shrugged. "There's not much to tell. My mum and dad came here near the end of the Irish potato famine. Eighteen fifty-nine, I think it was. They settled on the Lower East Side in one of the lung blocks. Four of my older brothers and sisters—I was the youngest of eight kids—died of TB. Another brother was killed during the Spanish American War. Both my parents are long since dead, but two of my sisters are still alive. One is a nun. The other one—she's only two years older than me—lives in Queens. She's married and has got five kids. At least it was five the last I heard."

She gave a forced-looking smile. "Don't look like that, honey. It wasn't all so bad as it sounds. I used to have a good time as a kid. I was sort of a tomboy, see, and I'd go over to the East River to fish off the docks. And we'd get out in the streets, dodging in and out through the pushcarts, and play kick the can—"

She was still describing street games of her childhood when the door opened and a man walked into the room, carrying a paper bag in one hand. He looked at Amanda and me with startled eyes and said, "What the hell!"

"Hank!" Rose Shannon's voice held both reproof and warning. She stood up. "What do you mean, barging in like this?"

"What do you mean, what do I mean barging— Oh, I get it!" He grinned. "Sorry, ma'am. I know I should of knocked. But I forgot."

He was a thin man, an inch or so over six feet, and good-looking in a street-corner-lounger sort of way. Dark sideburns showed beneath the straw hat he had not removed. He had large brown eyes, sharp but regular features, and a cleft in his chin.

Rose Shannon said, in a stiff voice, "This is Hank Dunkerly. He lives upstairs."

The man was staring at Amanda. "Okay. So you've told them who I am. Now tell me who they are."

I became aware that Rose Shannon's face held not only embarrassment but growing alarm. She said, "This is Miss Dorrance and Miss Hoffman."

"Hoffsteader."

"Miss Hoffsteader. They're friends of mine."

His grin widened. "Friends of yours since when?" His gaze moved from Amanda's face to Rose Shannon's. "She's the kid you mention sometimes when you're crying drunk, isn't she?"

Rose Shannon opened her mouth as if to deny it. Then, apparently aware that her expression had already betrayed her, she said nothing.

"Well, well, well! You never even told me her name, let alone that she was such a knockout. And such a dresser!" His gaze traveling from her toque ornamented with a glossy bird's wing to her handmade shoes, held the same sort of speculation I had seen in the detective's eyes as he looked around him in the Dorrance house.

Hank Dunkerly removed a bottle, filled with dark amber liquid, from the paper bag and held it aloft. "Okay, ladies. How about a drink?"

Rose Shannon's voice was sharp. "They don't want a drink. And neither do I."

"Then why the hell did you send me out for a fresh bottle?" When she didn't answer he shrugged and said, "I hope nobody minds if I have one."

He walked into the kitchen. After a moment came the sound of gurgling liquid. Rose Shannon said in a nervous voice, "Hank lives upstairs. Oh! I told you that already, didn't I?"

Filled glass in hand, he came back into the room. He had put his hat down someplace. I saw that his hair was thick and wavy. He sat down on a straight chair beneath the gas jet, took a long swallow of his drink, and smiled at Amanda.

"Rose never told me your name. Just said she'd had a

kid who'd been adopted. Didn't even say where you were now, and I didn't ask. Didn't like having her brood, you understand."

I could imagine the impatience he must have felt, listening to a drunken woman talk about the child she had given up.

"But now that I've met you— What's your name again?"

Amanda said crisply, "Dorrance. Amanda Dorrance."

He took another swallow. "Couldn't be you were adopted by John Dorrance, could it?"

I should not have been surprised. Although John Dorrance was not as famous as J. P. Morgan, his name was fairly well-known to the general public.

Amanda said in that same crisp voice, "Yes, Mr. and Mrs. John Dorrance adopted me."

He drank again and then said, "Holy Toledo! What a tub of butter you fell into."

"Hank, didn't you say you had to see a fellow about— about some sort of business?"

He looked at Rose and then laughed. "Okay, okay." He stood up, drained the rest of his drink, and set the glass down beside the kewpie doll on the mantel above the fake fireplace. "Nice to have met you, Miss Dorrance. And you too, Miss—Miss—"

"Hoffsteader."

"Well, so long." He opened the door into the hall and then closed it behind him.

For perhaps half a minute after he left there was silence in the room. Then Rose said, "The reason Hank acts so informal is that he's my fiancé, sort of.

"And he's a nice fellow," she went on, when neither of

us spoke. Her voice was nervously bright. "A little rough, but nice. And he's awfully smart. He's on his uppers right now, but he used to make a lot of money in the carnival business. Just as soon as he gets enough cash, he's going to start a new carnival. It'll travel all over the northeast to county fairs, and Elks and Masons benefits, and that sort of thing."

Amanda said, "How—how interesting."

Rose Shannon's fixed little smile wavered and broke. She said quietly, "It's been wonderful to see you, honey. But don't come here again. Please don't. Just forget you ever found me.

"And now," she added, getting to her feet, "I think you'd better go before—"

She didn't finish the sentence, but I knew what she meant. She wanted us to leave before Hank Dunkerly came back.

Amanda and I stood up. I think she welcomed the suggestion that we leave this frowzy flat. I know I did.

Rose Shannon said, "And remember. Don't let that poor woman—Don't let Mrs. Dorrance know that her husband—"

"I won't." Amanda stood there hesitantly for a moment and then leaned forward and kissed Rose Shannon's cheek. "Goodbye."

We didn't speak as we descended the narrow stairs. Even after we emerged into the sunlight we remained silent. We had to walk almost to Sixth Avenue along that drab street, drawing the gaze of shawled women and of men in blue work shirts and dungarees, before we found a hansom cab. As soon as we were inside it, Amanda burst into tears. I could not know just why she wept—whether because Rose Shannon was a drunken slattern, or because of John Dorrance's long deception, or for other reasons—and so I did not try to comfort her, but just let her cry it out.

Finally she wiped her eyes and put her handkerchief back in her pocket. "It's not so disgraceful, having been a dancer at the Haymarket. It's not like having been—having been—"

"No, of course it's not."

"And she's nice. It's for my sake that she doesn't want me to come there again. And look how she feels about Mother, the one I've always called Mother, I mean. Rose doesn't want to see her hurt."

I nodded, and then ventured, "Another good thing is that you found out that your father is your real father. Doesn't that please you?"

"I'm not so sure that it does! I think it awful of him to have neglected her all these years, except for sending money each month. Yes, I know she must spend a lot of it on—spirits, and maybe on that dreadful man. But my father should have had someone watching out for her, someone who'd report to him that she was living in a terrible place, and needed more money. He could have afforded it!

"And then there's Michael. How dare my father sneer at Michael for being Irish, when his own daughter is half Irish?"

I decided it was best not to try to answer. The cab, moving through increasingly heavy late afternoon traffic, finally left us at our door. Amanda and I went to our separate rooms. Something—perhaps the closeness of the air in that sleazy flat—had given me a headache.

Until six-thirty I lay down with a washcloth soaked in cold water over my eyes.

Amanda and I were in the kitchen, preparing a sketchy meal of cheese omelet and green salad, when the phone rang. Amanda went to answer it. She came back looking worried. "It's your father. I hope nothing's wrong."

Something was wrong. "Now don't worry," my father said. "Your mother's had a little dizzy spell. The doctor says she's just been overdoing. You know how she is. Practically ran the whole church bazaar on Wednesday, and gave a buffet luncheon for thirty of those Browning Society ladies yesterday. But if you could come home for a little while."

"Tell her I'm on my way."

As I hung up I realized that even though I was worried about Mother, I was glad to have an excuse to turn away for a while from my reckless friend, and from all the Dorrances with their secrets, their half-suppressed antagonisms and envies.

I turned and saw Amanda standing in the hall. "My mother is not well. It's nothing serious, apparently, but I'd better go home."

"Oh, I'm sorry."

"Do you think you can get Mrs. Nesbitt to come back right away?"

"Of course. I'll send a telegram. From Baltimore to New York is only an overnight train ride."

"Good." I could have added, "Then except for tonight you won't be alone here while you're having your dental work done." But during the last few days she had not once mentioned those coming sessions with the dentist. She might even have forgotten the excuse she had used to come to New York.

She said, "I'll miss you."

Probably she would. Certainly she had wanted my company to sustain her during her interview with the detective and during her visit to Rose Shannon. But I felt that now she, as well as I, welcomed the thought of separation. Now she could be with Michael as often as she pleased without having to face, afterward, my unspoken but obvious disapproval.

"I'll miss you, too," I said, and hurried upstairs to pack.

9

As always when I returned from either of the Dorrance houses to Brooklyn, I found the atmosphere of my parents' home as comforting as a warm bath. Although confined to bed for a week, my mother seemed as cheerful and healthy-looking as ever. I spent several hours a day at her bedside, playing two-handed bridge, or just talking while we both knitted squares of the afghan bedspread that we had been making, off and on, for the previous two years. The rest of the time I supervised our cook and two housemaids, read, played chess with my father, and walked along Brooklyn Heights, inhaling the salt air from the open sea and admiring the massed buildings on the Manhattan shore.

My second afternoon at home, Amanda telephoned. As if to prove to me that the housekeeper had returned, she called Mrs. Nesbitt to the phone, and she, too, inquired about my mother.

A week passed. Worried about Amanda, I called the Fifth Avenue house. Mrs. Nesbit told me that Miss Amanda was in her bath but would call back. Half an hour later she did call.

We chatted for a while. Then I asked, "Is your dental work finished?"

After a moment she said, "Yes. The dentist managed to save the tooth."

"Then I guess you'll be going back to East Hampton."

Again she was silent for a few seconds. Then she said, "Why should I? I've gotten so I can't stand that house. It's like a morgue. Mother keeps to her rooms most of the time, and Lucy practically hates me, and Larry either has his nose in a book or is talking in some corner with Lucy. Why, I get more companionship out of Mrs. Nesbitt."

I wanted to say, it isn't the housekeeper's companionship that keeps you in New York. Instead I said, "Amanda, Mrs. Dorrance is going to be very upset if you don't join her in East Hampton."

"Ha! That's all you know. I telephoned her last night. She said that I must be out of my mind, wanting to stay here when I could be sea bathing and playing tennis in East Hampton. But if New York in the summer was my idea of pleasure, she said, I could stay here."

Even if Mrs. Dorrance was that indifferent to Amanda's actions, I thought, surely she should not be indifferent to the social disgrace her headstrong adopted daughter might bring upon the family name. True, most of the people in the Dorrance's circle spent their summers out in the Hamptons, or in Colorado, or Europe. But there must be a few people in town who knew Amanda, and might see her going into Michael's building on Central Park South, or even coming out of his apartment.

Then another thought struck me. If Mrs. Dorrance knew that her husband had palmed off his illegitimate child upon her—and I was almost certain she did know—then perhaps she hated him enough so she actually hoped that the Dorrance name might be disgraced, disgraced by the daughter he preferred to his legitimate children. Even if Mrs. Dorrance had not admitted that hope to her full consciousness, it might still be there, impelling her to consent to Amanda's long stay in the Fifth Avenue house, supervised only by a servant.

I said, "Please, Amanda. Please go out to East Hampton."

After a long moment she said, "Emma, one would think you were twenty years older than I, instead of several weeks younger. Now why don't you concentrate on your own life, instead of worrying about mine?"

Her tone made the implication clear. Having been unable to attract a man, I really didn't have a life of my own to concentrate upon.

I said, hurt and indignant, "Just a few days ago you wanted me to be concerned. But very well. From now on I'll take no interest in what you do. Goodbye, Amanda."

She rang back in less than ten minutes, all contrition. I was her best friend, maybe her only real friend, and she not only wanted my interest. She needed it. Could I forgive her for what she'd said?

I replied, coolly, that I forgave her. I was still more than a little distant with her when she phoned the next day, ostensibly to learn how my mother was. But during subsequent conversations I found I could not maintain my air of aloof dignity. I was still fond of my reckless and generous friend, even though falling in love had made her careless at times of other people's feelings.

But although we had friendly telephone chats two or three times a week, she did not invite me to the Fifth Avenue house, or even suggest that we have lunch someplace. I'm sure she was afraid that if we had a prolonged conversation face to face, one of its topics undoubtedly would be her reason for staying in town despite the July heat.

My mother had resumed her household and social activities. Near the end of July she and I and my father attended a concert given by the German-American Lieder Society in a downtown Brooklyn hall. Carl Bauer—"young Dr. Bauer"—was there, seated across the aisle from us, and beaming at me through his glasses. When the concert was over he and I, punch cups in hand, chatted at the rear of the hall. He told me that I was looking fit and then said that yes, he had been going out to the Hamptons each weekend.

"Everyone misses you, Emma."

"Well, I miss the people I know out there. Have you seen any of the Dorrances?"

"Not Mr. Dorrance, of course. He's still in Europe. But I've seen the twins around town. And last Sunday I talked to Mrs. Dorrance at a lawn party."

"Did she say anything about Amanda?" I had not talked to my friend for almost a week. For all I knew, she might have finally decided to rejoin her family.

"Oh, just that she's still in town."

Embarrassment was in his voice and in the blue-gray

eyes behind the heavy lenses. So what I had feared had happened. Someone in New York, someone who knew Amanda, had found out about her and Michael Doyle. And now the story was all over the Hamptons.

Had it reached Clara Dorrance's ears? Perhaps not. But perhaps it had. I could imagine her waiting, cold face composed, to tell her husband upon his return that his daughter had been going to bed with "the Irish saloonkeeper's son."

Someone touched my arm. I turned to see my father standing there. He said, with his heavy accent, "Good evening, Dr. Bauer. Will you excuse Emma now? Her mama wants to go home."

A few days later my father left his factory in the care of his chief assistant and accompanied my mother and me to an Adirondack resort for a month-long vacation. Even though I preferred the seashore, I enjoyed the walks along mountain trails, and canoeing on the lake, and gathering with other hotel guests at night around a campfire to sing "Yankee Doodle" and "Put on Your Old Gray Bonnet."

Most of all, during the last two weeks of August, I enjoyed the company of my cousin Paul Miller. Because his mother—my mother's sister—had died when he was very young, Paul frequently had stayed with my parents and me when his father's work as a civil engineer took him to other parts of the country. Consequently I had grown up thinking of Paul as almost a brother, an exceedingly nice brother who frequently protected and seldom teased.

At twenty-two, and fresh out of M.I.T., Paul was tall

and blond and very good-looking, so much so that the girls at the resort competed for his attention. He took obvious pleasure in dancing and flirting with them, but he also spent time with me, laughing about incidents of our childhood, and talking of his future as a member of his father's engineering firm.

I had sent Amanda a postcard soon after our arrival at the resort, but had received no communication from her. Consequently I was a little surprised when, about ten minutes after my parents and I returned to the Brooklyn house, Amanda telephoned me.

Her voice was tense. "Your card said you'd be back today. I've been telephoning ever since early this afternoon."

"Amanda, what is it?"

"I'm in East Hampton. Papa is coming home a few days from now, and Michael is coming to see him. Please, Emma, I need you. Please come out here."

"Why is Michael—"

"He's coming to tell Papa we want to be married, of course."

Her voice had risen. Anyone passing the door of her room could have heard her. And also, I reflected, Mrs. Dorrance could be listening on the phone in her sitting room. Or Lucy, wearing her cat's smile, could be listening on the phone in the downstairs hall.

"Amanda, I've decided to accept Miss Farnsworth's offer to have me assist her at the school this year. That means that between now and the time school opens I'll have to shop for suitable clothes and—"

"Please, Emma. Stay with me if only for a few days. Please. I need you."

Much as I had enjoyed past summers in that lovely East Hampton mansion, I felt almost a revulsion at the thought of going out there now. But Amanda certainly would need me. If her and Michael's encounter with her father ended in the sort of debacle I feared, Amanda would get no comfort from other members of that strange household.

"All right," I said. "I'll come."

10

At the East Hampton station the next day, I stepped from the train into the warm sunlight of late afternoon. Thorsen, the Dorrances' gardener-caretaker, was waiting for me. He explained that Halloran, the young chauffeur who also kept the Dorrances' Pierce-Arrow and their electric brougham in repair, had broken his arm. In the Pierce-Arrow we drove down Newtown Lane, with its twin rows of shops, and then across Main Street. It was still thronged with summer traffic, carriages and buggies and farm wagons and bicycles and motor cars.

Thorsen had opened the glass pane between the chauffeur and passenger compartments, something he would not have done, I felt, if he'd been driving a member of the Dorrance family. While we were moving along a curving road east of Main Street, I said, "Mr. Dorrance is not home yet?"

"No, Miss Emma. As I understand it, he will land in New York next Thursday."

"How is the rest of the family?"

"They seem much as usual."

"Including Miss Amanda?"

After a moment he answered, "I really couldn't say, miss. I've caught only a few glimpses of her since she came back from New York."

Always when he spoke of his employer's elder daughter his tone was remote. But now it sounded so cold that I wondered if rumors about how Amanda had spent her summer had reached him too.

He asked, "And you, Miss Emma? How have you been?"

"Just fine, thank you."

"Are you getting ready to go back to school?"

"In a way. Not to study. I was graduated last June. But I'm to be assistant to the head mistress at the Bradley School. Later on I may go to teacher's college and get my certificate."

"A teacher," he said warmly. "That's a fine thing for a woman to be. Your parents must be very proud."

"I hope they are pleased with me."

I felt a wry pity. Plainly he had been so shattered by his beautiful daughter's fall from virtue that he envied the parents of girls like me, girls who, unafflicted by the attentions of men, were free to devote their lives to teaching other people's children.

As we neared the Dorrance gates I saw evidence, in the form of a man named Orren Creavey, that summer officially was over, despite the fully-leafed trees and traffic-clogged Main Street. Orren was one of the three men the Goddard Lane Property Association paid to patrol past their elaborate summer homes twenty-four hours a day, from early September until June. Orren, who had the four to midnight shift, was peddling toward us on his bicycle. His jacket was open on this warm afternoon, showing the gun belt strapped around his thickening waist. With a smile on his broad, middle-aged face, he waved to us as he passed.

The gates were open. Thorsen stopped at the foot of the drive and carried my valise up the front steps. The housemaid who opened the door took the valise and then said to me, "Miss Amanda is expecting you, miss. She asked that you go straight up to her room. I'll put your valise in your room."

As soon as I had entered Amanda's room she threw herself, weeping, into my arms. I asked, patting her shoulder, "What is it?"

"It's just that I'm so glad to see you," she wailed. Then, almost in the same breath: "And I'm so worried!"

"Tell me about it."

We sat down on the bed's edge. She mopped her face with a handkerchief, blew her nose. She was paler than she usually was at this time of year, which wasn't surprising. After all, she'd spent the summer in the city. But what did surprise and alarm me were the dark circles under her eyes, and her thinness.

"You don't look well."

"I haven't been sleeping much lately. It's worry about what my father is going to say or do. Why, he may not even consent to see Michael. And he's got to. Michael and I are more in love than ever. Oh, we could run away and get married. But why should we do that, as if—as if there was something shameful in our marriage, as if Michael wasn't good enough for me? He is good enough, more than good enough, and Papa has to admit it."

88

"Have you and Michael thought of ways to convince him?"

"Michael is going to bring some sort of papers out here—balance sheets, I think he called them— to show how well Matthew Doyle Enterprises is doing. As soon as we are married, it will be Matthew Doyle and Son Enterprises. You see, Michael has worked hard in his father's main office all summer, and he'll go on working hard."

With a pang I thought of Michael saying, "I'd planned to paint pictures." Well, obviously he thought marriage to Amanda was worth the sacrifice of those plans. In fact, he'd said so that night last June.

"Don't you think that may convince Papa? Don't you?"

I did not. No consideration of Michael's economic prospects, I felt sure, would sway John Dorrance. To him the Doyles would remain Irish saloonkeepers, no matter how rich they might become. But perhaps he might be swayed by the fact that after a whole summer Amanda was still in love with Michael. Probably John Dorrance had sailed for Europe confident that in a week or two Amanda, surrounded.as she was by an ever-growing group of admirers, would forget about that Doyle fellow.

I said, "I think there's a chance your father will say yes, even a good chance. Now I think I'll bathe and change. After that train ride I feel gritty with coal dust."

My room had an attached bath. It was one of the smaller of the seven bathrooms in the house. Its tub, nearly large enough to have accommodated President Taft, stretched almost from wall to wall. After I had bathed, I put on a blue linen skirt and a white lawn shirtwaist with a blue linen tie. I went out into the hall, and then hesitated, knowing that good manners required that I notify Mrs. Dorrance of my presence, and yet reluctant to see her. Finally I turned and walked toward her sitting room and bedroom in the west wing. I knocked, and her voice called, "Come in."

I found her stretched out on a chaise longue, a magazine in her hand. Sunset light, pouring through the west windows, gave her face a spurious look of health. She said, laying the magazine on a wicker table beside her, "Hello, Emma. Forgive me for not getting up. This is one of my bad days." She gestured toward a wicker armchair. "Please sit down."

When I was seated I said, "If I should have received an invitation directly from you, I apologize. But I gathered from Amanda—"

"Oh, Emma. As Amanda's closest friend, you are practically a member of the family. Speaking of families, how are your parents?"

For several minutes we talked about my mother and father, and the month I had spent with them in the Adirondacks. In turn, she told me about some of the private parties and charity events that had taken place in the Hamptons during the summer.

Finally I said, "I hear that Mr. Dorrance is returning soon."

"His boat docks Thursday morning."

Her thin face had lighted with pleasure. But it was not the pleasure of a woman about to be reunited with a beloved husband. There was something almost fierce in it.

I thought, feeling chilled, she's looking forward to the explosion she knows will occur between her husband and Amanda.

True, John Dorrance would also be furious with his wife when he learned that she had consented to his daughter's staying in the Fifth Avenue house all summer. But as a semi-invalid, Mrs. Dorrance would have a means of countering his charge that she had been delinquent in her maternal duties. She could say that curbing a headstrong girl like Amanda had been too much for her.

She said, "I'm sorry I won't see you at dinner tonight. I'm having a tray sent up."

With relief, I took that as my cue to leave. I said, standing up, "Goodbye for now. I hope you feel better tomorrow."

I left her and went down the stairs. I felt too restless to return to my room, and too weary at the moment to seek Amanda's distraught company. I would select a book from the library, go out onto the terrace, and read in the lingering daylight until the dinner gong sounded.

On the ground floor I walked back along the hall to the library. The electric lamp with its Tiffany shade of multicolored glass was burning on the long refectory table. Nevertheless, I had taken a couple of steps past the threshold before I saw that Larry Dorrance stood in one corner of the book-lined room. I said, "Oh, excuse me. I didn't know I would be disturbing anyone."

"You're not disturbing me." A book in his hands, he gave me his pleasant and yet distant smile. "Did you come out on the afternoon train?"

"That's right."

"Are you looking for something to read until dinner?" His voice took on a certain animation. But then, the only extended conversations with Larry which I could remember were about books. He reached up to a shelf. "Here's Theodore Dreiser's *Sister Carrie*. It's a fine novel. Ever hear of it?"

"Yes. Wasn't it suppressed when it first came out?"

"Yes, by some bunch of idiots or another. But it's back in print." He handed the book to me. "I think you'll like it, but keep it in your room. If my father sees it, he'll burst a blood vessel." He added bitterly, "Not that he isn't sure to burst one anyway."

I felt startled. Until now I had felt that Larry, withdrawn from everything except his twin, would not be interested in troubles between Amanda and their father. I said, "You mean because Amanda—"

I broke off. He blinked and said, "Amanda? This has nothing to do with Amanda. It's me. I don't want to enter Princeton two weeks from now, and I won't."

"That will cause a row!" A Princeton graduate himself, John Dorrance was determind that his son go there, however short he might fall of his father's brilliant athletic record. "Where do you want to go?"

"Harvard. Even if I have to wait until the second semester to get in, I want to go to Harvard."

I wondered, why Harvard? Then I realized the probable reason. He did not want to be separated from the one person he felt close to, his twin. Lucy had passed Wellesley College's entrance examination and soon would enroll there. Although Larry, if he went to Princeton, could come home for weekends, Lucy would not be able to travel from Massachusetts to New York

92

except for Christmas and Easter and summer vacations. But if Larry went to Harvard, less than ten miles from the Wellesley campus, he could see his sister frequently.

He looked past my shoulder, his face lighting up. Knowing whom I would see, I turned around. Lucy was walking into the room. She stopped two or three feet away from me and said, "Hello, Emma. So you've come to visit us again."

Commonplace words. But as usual she accompanied them with that little smile which seemed to say that she was recalling something about the person she addressed, something both amusing and discreditable.

"Hello, Lucy," I said. "Well, if you'll excuse me now . . . "

I felt both of them watching me as I left the room.

11

Amanda and I were together most of our waking hours for the next two days. We went to the beach club, where the crowd on the terrace had thinned considerably, now that it was September. Although she did not seem to be able to keep her mind on either game, we played tennis on the court near the greenhouse and Russian bank up in the tower room.

And Amanda talked. And talked and talked. About herself and Michael, of course. No other topic held her attention for more than a few seconds. She told me that already they had gone flat-hunting, and decided that after they were married they would live in one of the new buildings on the Upper West Side. She told me that Michael had bought a motor car, a small red two-seater of the sort called a runabout. She told me that she intended to study cookbooks, especially recipes for Michael's favorite dishes, so that she could run the flat with the help of only a twice-a-week cleaning woman, and thus save money to be reinvested in Matthew Doyle and Son. She told me that she and Michael planned that sometime within the next few years they would visit the Irish village where Doyles had lived for centuries. And she told me each of these things not once but several times, chattering on and on feverishly.

John Dorrance's ship was to dock at eight Thursday morning. So as to meet his employer as soon as he cleared customs, Thorsen drove to New York in the Pierce-Arrow the night before. Shortly before noon on Thursday I bicycled to Southampton and had a solitary lunch at the Irving Hotel. If I did not want to be present when Mr. Dorrance was united with his troubled family, and I certainly did not, then it behooved me to stay away until late afternoon. After lunch, leaving my bicycle in the hotel's rack, I wandered up and down Southampton's Main Street, looking in shop windows and entering a few that offered end-of-season sales. I bought a camisole in Hildreth's Department Store, and from a bookshop Jack London's latest novel, *Burning Daylight*. Around four I went to the hotel for my bicycle and then pedaled through the golden September light, past farmhouses and fields of corn and cauliflower, to East Hampton.

I left my bicycle in the rack beside the carriage-house garage. Its door was open. I looked in and saw the Pierce-Arrow standing between the electric brougham and the closed carriage which the family still sometimes used. Carrying my purchases, I went around to the front of the house and climbed the steps. I found the house quiet, ominously so.

I climbed the stairs to my room. I had just placed my book on a table and my camisole in a drawer when someone knocked. It was Edith. "Miss Emma, Mr. Dorrance would be pleased if you came down to his study."

Nerves tight, I descended the stairs and walked back along the hall to a door next to the library. I knocked, and Mr. Dorrance's voice told me to come in. I entered the fairly large room, with its desk bare of everything except an ivory-handled letter opener and onyx-based pen and inkwell set; its steel safe; and its shelves of reference books. John Dorrance stood beside the un-lighted fireplace. "Hello, Emma. You're looking well." His smile held that easy charm he could summon up whenever he wanted to. He waved to one of the two leather armchairs flanking the fireplace. "Please sit down."

He remained standing. He said, in a very different voice, "I'll get right to the point. You know that Amanda spent the summer in New York, don't you." It was a statement, not a question.

I made the little speech I had framed as I descended the stairs. "Mr. Dorrance, Amanda is my friend. Do you think it is fair to question me about her?"

He gave a grim little smile. "To ease your conscience, I will tell you that Thorsen, Mrs. Dorrance, and Amanda herself have already told me that she was there all summer. You were with her for about a week. The rest of the time she was alone except for the housekeeper."

Nerves taut, I waited for him to say that Amanda also had told him about her affair with Michael. But he didn't say it, and after a moment I realized that of course Amanda would not have told him about that, not

96

yet, anymore than she would have told him about our visit to Rose Shannon. Amanda was hoping that Michael would win her father over. The last thing she would want to do would be to anger her father more than necessary ahead of time.

He said, "No, Emma, I didn't ask you down here to tattle on Amanda. What I want is your opinion. Do you think my daughter's feeling for this fellow is really serious? Or is she doing this just to spite me?"

Without giving me a chance to reply, he went on in a brooding voice, "Children! You do your best for them, and yet they grow up wanting to hurt you, even if in the process they ruin their own lives."

"Mr. Dorrance, I don't think that's true of Amanda. I think she really loves Michael Doyle."

After a moment he said, in a flat voice, "I'm sorry to hear that, because she's just going to have to get over it. I'm not going to let her ruin—Emma, did you know that the first American Dorrance, who came here fifty years before the Revolution, was a cabinetmaker's apprentice? Through brains and hard work and yes, luck, we've risen in the generations since then, not just to an unassailable financial position but to a social one as well. I'll be damned if I'll let a silly girl ruin all that."

I summoned up the courage to contradict him. "I realize that if she marries Michael she'll be dropped from the Social Register. But probably her entire family won't be. The Van Rysicks weren't dropped, even though Alice Van Rysick eloped with their head gardener's son."

"And you think it was all right for Alice to do that, do you?"

"If—if they really loved each other."

"Emma! I've always considered you far too sensible to talk such romantic twaddle. Do you know what happened a year after that elopement? The gardener's son deserted her, probably because he got tired of waiting for her family to forgive her and start handing her money. She's living in Italy now, on a small allowance her family sends. I hear she's twice attempted suicide.

"No, Emma, young people have their best chance of happiness when they choose a mate from their own background. Not that it guarantees happiness, God knows." I was sure that he was thinking of himself and Clara Dorrance. "But at least they have a far better chance than in one of these storybook princess-and-the-stableboy marriages."

Privately I agreed with him. But in Amanda and Michael's case there was a factor he apparently did not know about, that summer-long affair of theirs. It was a factor which, at least in my opinion, made it important that they marry.

I said, "I don't think it's right to compare Amanda and Michael to Alice Van Rysick and the man she married. Michael isn't poor, or a fortune hunter. He loves her. He told me so, and I believe him."

Again he gave me that grim little smile. "And so your advice is?"

"Let them marry, with your blessing."

"No, Emma. She'll just have to get over it."

I said, after a moment, "Are you going to see him?"

"Yes. He telephoned an hour ago. He's coming here tomorrow night at eight o'clock."

Then all was not lost, not necessarily. Surely others

besides Amanda—and I!—were susceptible to Michael's appealing qualities. Surely he would not fail to win John Dorrance's respect, however grudging. And that would be the first step.

I said, "Will you excuse me now? It's about time to dress for dinner."

Once more he was all courtesy. "Of course, Emma. And thank you for discussing this with me."

Dinner that night was a highly uncomfortable meal. John Dorrance ignored Amanda and concentrated his attention upon Lucy. He asked her if she was ready to go up to Wellesley, what her first semester courses would be, and what residence hall she would live in. No doubt pleased that he did not even look at Amanda, who sat there silently spooning chilled consommé, Lucy made her demure replies.

Suddenly he turned to Larry. "And you, Lawrence. Are you all set to go to Princeton?"

Larry's fair skin flushed. "I would rather not talk about it right now, sir."

John Dorrance geniality vanished. "Not talk about it! What is there to talk about? Are you all set to enter Princeton, or aren't you? A simple yes or no will suffice."

"Then it's no."

The knuckles of the hand with which John Dorrance held his spoon whitened, but his voice remained fairly even. "Why is it no?"

"Because I want to go to Harvard instead."

"Harvard!" he said, after a long moment. "Why on earth should you want to go to Harvard? If you planned to go into law I could understand it, but as it is—"

He broke off, and then said with a smile, "Is it because Cambridge is not far from Wellesley? I know you've always felt close to your sister. But you're both almost grown up now, with separate lives to lead."

"Please, sir, if we could talk about it later on."

"Very well. But all the Dorrances go to Princeton. And unless you can come up with some very convincing arguments, that is where you are going."

After dinner I played rummy with Amanda in her room, or rather, I played. She seemed to drop cards almost at random, not minding that I won trick after trick. And she kept up a stream of repetitious talk. When she had said for perhaps the fourth time, "I know he will talk Papa around tomorrow night, I just know he will," I realized that my nerves were about to snap. Saying that I wanted to get a letter off to Miss Farnsworth, my future employer, in the morning mail, I went to my room.

The next day after lunch, thinking that physical activity might distract her, I suggested to Amanda that we play tennis. When she rejected the idea I said, "Well, I feel the need for exercise. I think I'll bat balls against the carriage house for a while."

I had been out there about twenty minutes, batting a tennis ball against the carriage house wall, when Mr. Dorrance appeared, racket in hand. "Like to play a couple of sets, Emma?"

Perhaps he felt he had appeared harsh and discourteous during our talk the day before, and wanted to make up for it. Whatever the reason for his offer to play, I welcomed it.

We went onto the court. John Dorrance was past fifty then. What's more, I was considered a good player. But he won both sets easily. As we were putting our rackets into their covers he asked, "Are Thorsen's autumn crocuses in bloom yet?"

The crocus beds lay beyond a tall yew hedge at the far end of the reflecting pool. "I don't know. I haven't been back there."

"Shall we look for them now?"

We walked back along the rectangular pool, between the rows of statuary and the lines of rose bushes, some of them bearing their second blooms of the season. But I can't to this day remember whether or not the crocuses were in bloom, because when we went through the gate in the yew hedge to the little garden beyond, we saw Lawrence and Lucy. They sat on a stone bench against the hedge that walled the garden on the east. One hand holding a book, the other arm draped over Lucy's shoulder, he was reading aloud to her. I recognized a line from Wordsworth's "The Solitary Reaper."

John Dorrance stopped short. I turned and looked at his stunned face. And I felt that I could read his sudden, devastating conviction, almost as clearly as if he had spoken it aloud.

I've been sure through all the years since that it was a mistaken conviction. Oh, there was something not quite healthy in the twins' close attachment to each other, just at an age when they both should have been making friends with increasing numbers of young people. But I am sure there was nothing overtly incestuous in their relationship.

101

They had seen us now. They sat motionless, puzzled alarm in their faces, as John Dorrance advanced upon them. I stood rooted to the spot.

He seized the book Larry held and hurled it down the walk. "Lucy, go in the house! No, not you, sir. You sit right there."

For once not smiling her sly little smile, Lucy turned a frightened face toward me for a moment as she walked through the gate in the hedge.

John Dorrance was saying, "You're not going to Harvard, you—you—You're not even going to Princeton. V.M.I. is where you're going. That's right. The Virginia Military Institute."

I found I was able to move. I went through the gate in the hedge. But even as I hurried down the walk beside the pool, I could still hear John Dorrance's raised voice. "They know how to handle all kinds there! If you don't measure up, they'll put you on the parade ground and march you up and down until you drop."

I felt sorry for Larry, and even for Lucy. But I was even sorrier for Amanda and Michael. Because he was enraged at his own son, there was even less chance than ever that, a few hours from now, he would give a fair hearing to the "Irish saloonkeeper's son."

12

How many members of the family gathered in the dining room that night I cannot say, because I was not there. As soon as I reached my room after witnessing that ugly scene in the garden, I wrote a short note, saying that I had arranged to dine with "some friends of my parents" in East Hampton. Then I rang for Edith. I gave her the note, along with the request that she give it to Mr. or Mrs. Dorrance, "sometime before dinner." After that I went into the hall, praying that Amanda would not come out of her room. She did not.

I slipped out the front door. Because I feared that I might encounter Mr. Dorrance or Larry if I got my bicycle from the rack beside the carriage house, I walked the mile to East Hampton's Main Street.

I went to the public library first and stayed there, browsing through a history of Long Island, until closing time. Then I walked north on Main Street to a drugstore and soda parlor on Newtown Lane. Seated at a marble-topped table, I consumed a ham sandwich and vanilla soda. I had almost finished my sketchy meal when I heard the evening train from the city, its whistle blowing, pull into the station a few hundred yards away. I wished heartily that the train was headed in the other direction and that I was aboard it.

The days had grown shorter. At only a little past six, the light was fading. I paid the pharmacist, walked back along Main Street, and then turned onto Goddard Lane. Now that the sun was down, the air had an early fall crispness. I walked at a brisk pace past the open fields and the summer houses of the rich, set well back behind tall hedges or stone walls.

As Amanda's closest friend, I long since had been accorded the privilege of entering the East Hampton house without ringing. I heard no sound but my own footsteps as I crossed the hall to the stairs.

I was about to enter my own room when Amanda opened her door and came out into the hall. "Emma! I'm so glad you're back."

"I thought you might be asleep, and so I left without disturbing you. I'd forgotten to tell you that these friends of my parents—"

"I know," she said impatiently. "Edith told me."

She caught my hand and drew me into her room. She sat down on the edge of the bed, hands clasped tightly in her lap, and I sat in a wicker armchair.

I said, "Michael is still coming here at eight?"

"Yes. He telephoned me early this afternoon. He thinks it will be better if he doesn't even ask to see me tonight, at least not until after he and Papa have had their talk. That's wise, don't you think? I mean, it will help put Papa in a good mood."

I had a feeling that where Michael Doyle was concerned her father's mood could never be good, and

104

especially not tonight. Did she know about the rage his son had awakened in him only that afternoon? Probably not. Neither Larry nor Lucy would be apt to mention it to her. Anyway, I certainly wasn't going to tell her.

I looked at the tray sitting on her dressing table. It held an empty coffee cup and a plate of roast beef, yellow squash, and green beans. She had taken a bite or two of the slice of roast beef, but the rest of the food appeared untouched.

"So you had your dinner brought up."

"Yes. I was afraid that if I went to the dining room I might do or say something to irritate Papa, so I sent down a note saying I had a headache. I guess that was all right with him. At least he hasn't come storming up here."

"But you've eaten practically nothing!"

"I'll eat once I know that Papa is not going to try to keep us from getting married. Once I know that I'll eat and eat and sleep and sleep."

A silence settled down for several minutes. Then I heard the sound of an engine. The sound grew louder, as if a motor car was moving up the Dorrance drive. Suddenly paler than before, Amanda looked at the small onyx-framed clock on her dressing table. It was one that had always been there. Apparently even if John Dorrance had brought her the Swiss clock she had requested, he had not given it to her. She said, "One minute of eight. I told him how Papa always says that punctuality is the politeness of kings, whatever that means."

We heard the faint, distant shrilling of the doorbell. The house was too solidly built for us to hear the maid opening the front door, or anything she and Michael might have said to each other.

Again silence settled down, a more oppressive one than before. Amanda had stretched out on the bed, but there was nothing relaxed in her attitude. She stared at the ceiling, eyes enormous.

"Let me get something to read to you," I said. She did not protest. I went into my room, came back with *Sister Carrie,* and, sitting down, began to read aloud Dreiser's account of Carrie's search for work in the Chicago of twenty years before. Whether Amanda even heard me I don't know. Each time I glanced at her I saw that her expression had not changed.

Then we heard the shouts. Men's enraged shouts, so loud that they carried from the lower hall, up the stairs, and through the bedroom door. Amanda got off the bed, lunged for the doorknob. I went with her out into the hall. From downstairs came the slamming of a door—the study door, to judge by the direction of the sound.

Amanda and I had reached the landing. She screamed, "Michael!"

Hand on the front doorknob, Michael turned and looked up at her. His face under the curly dark hair was almost as white as hers. His dark blue eyes had a blind look. "It's no use. I'm going. I have to."

"Michael!" She descended a step and then, swaying, clutched the bannister. "What do you mean?"

"We can't see each other again. And if you want to know why, ask your son of a bitch of a father." He went out the front door and slammed it shut behind him.

Clinging to the bannister, Amanda descended

106

another step. I seized her arm. "Go to your room! I'll go after him and try to find out . . . Now go lie down, before you faint."

Face ashen, eyes dazed, she turned and began to climb. I ran down the stairs and out onto the veranda.

A first quarter moon had risen. It was bright enough that I could see a small motor car—black in that light, although I was sure it was red—drive out through the open gates and turn toward Main Street. Slowly I came back into the house.

"Emma."

I looked to my left. John Dorrance stood there. "Emma, please come into my study." Then, as I glanced up the stairs: "You can go up to her in a moment. In fact, there is something I want you to explain to her, since I'm in no mood to cope with her hysteria tonight."

I followed him into his study. On his desk lay a manila envelope. He picked it up and held it out to me. "Do you want to look through this?"

Even to my own ears my voice was cold. "Just tell me what it is."

Shrugging, he dropped the envelope onto his desk. "You probably wouldn't understand them anyway. These are due bills, or rather photographic copies of them. The originals are in one of my safety deposit boxes in New York."

"Due bills?"

"On Matthew Doyle's various assets. You see, he has been expanding very fast. For that he needed money, and so for these past few years he has been borrowing it in the form of demand loans, with all his assets as security for them—his house in New York and a growing number of bar concessions in Manhattan and Brooklyn."

I said, "And you loaned him this money?"

"Of course not. I didn't even know the fellow existed until his son . . . But anyway, I made it my business to find out about the Doyles. In the few days before I left for Europe I took the precaution of buying up all his paper. Because I was in a hurry, I had to pay a premium for some of it, but I bought it."

I understood then. I said, feeling sick, "And tonight—"

"Tonight I told Michael Doyle that if he ever tries to see Amanda again, his father will be out on the street, as broke as when he landed at Ellis Island."

I thought of the pride and affection with which Michael had spoken of his father, his understanding father who, even though he himself had risen from immigrant boy to prosperous entrepreneur, was willing for his only son to forsake business for canvas and paintbrush.

My voice shook. "How anyone can be so cruel—"

"Now, stop it, Emma." Perhaps because his victory was so complete, he sounded mild. "I'm no more cruel than a surgeon is when, to save a patient's life, he amputates a limb. I'm saving young Doyle as well as Amanda. Two years from now or maybe less she will be happily married to some man of her own kind. Michael Doyle will find a young woman suitable for him. And they will both have been saved a lifetime of unhappiness."

"I can only hope you're right."

I left the study, hurried up the stairs. When I reached the landing I caught a glimpse of movement to my right. I looked along the hall and saw Sara, the youngest of the housemaids, moving rapidly away from me, a pile of folded blankets in her arms. Had she been here in the second floor hall when Michael shouted his denunciation of John Dorrance? Perhaps. And even if she hadn't been, Michael's voice had been so loud that at least one or two of the servants must have heard him, and that meant by tomorrow they would all know about it. And within a few days scores of other people would know too.

I knocked on Amanda's door and heard her say, "Come in." Her voice sounded so weak that I forgot all about other people. I found her sitting on the floor, legs curled under her, her cheek and one extended arm resting on the counterpane.

"Amanda!"

She lifted her head. "I'm all right," she said in a weakly impatient voice. "I just felt dizzy for a moment. Now tell me—"

"No, I didn't get to talk to Michael. He'd already driven off. Now lie down."

I helped her onto the bed and then said, "I'm going to call the doctor."

Fear and protest in the violet eyes. "No!"

"But Amanda!"

"I'm all *right*."

I think I realized the truth then, but I turned my thoughts from it. The important thing was to have the doctor look at her. There was no point in upsetting her further, though, by making the call from her room. "I'll be back," I said.

As I descended the stairs I saw that John Dorrance

stood in the lower hall, as if debating whether or not to come to his daughter's room. I said, "Amanda fainted. And her color is very bad." It gave me satisfaction to see his own face lose color. "You'd better call Dr. Bauer." The Bauer house, also on Goddard Lane, was only a few hundred yards away. "And I don't think you should see her now. She's already very upset."

He turned toward his study. I climbed the stairs and went into Amanda's room. Her dark head turned on the pillow. "Have you talked to Papa?" Her voice was taut. "Did he tell you what he did to Michael to make him—make him—"

"Yes." Not knowing the cause of Michael's behavior, I felt, would distress her even more than knowing. I pulled a chair close to the bed, sat down, and told her.

She was silent for a long moment. Then she said bitterly, "Papa would do it, too. He would smash that good, generous man as if he were a bug."

"You've met Michael's father?"

"No, but Michael often talks about him. I know how much he loves his father and respects him. He would never let anyone or anything hurt . . ." Her voice trailed off wretchedly. Then she rallied. "But Michael and I will manage to see each other, someway, without Papa knowing. We'll work something out."

I said without conviction, "Of course you will."

She closed bruised-looking eyelids. I sat there, trying to tell myself that nothing ailed her except unhappiness. Then I heard the doorbell ring downstairs.

Moments later someone knocked. I opened the door, looked at young Dr. Bauer, and said, "Oh! I expected your father. But it's Friday night, isn't it, so of course you're out here." I looked past his shoulder, half expecting to see John Dorrance. But apparently I had managed to frighten him into staying downstairs.

I opened the door wide. Carl Bauer, bag in hand, came into the room. He said, in his formal, slightly European way, "Good evening, Amanda."

I said, "You'll be able to find me in my room. It's next door to this one."

In my room, too restless to read or even sit, I walked up and down. Except for my muffled footsteps and the shrilling of katydids in the trees outside my window, the night was still.

Someone knocked. I opened the door, and Dr. Bauer came into the room. I closed the door behind him and then looked up into his big face with its thick-lensed glasses. He looked not only distressed but embarrassed.

I decided to put an end to his qualms about breaking such news to an unmarried young woman. I said, "Amanda is going to have a baby, isn't she?"

After a moment he said, "Yes, she is. Some time in March, I'd say." He paused. "She told me to tell you."

"And her general health?"

"She's run-down, undoubtedly because she's been eating and sleeping too little. But I would say her health is basically sound."

I said, "Don't tell her parents about the baby."

"But her father is waiting downstairs. If he asks me what her condition is—"

"Say she's just run-down! Please. If I tell you what happened here tonight—"

I did tell him. From the look of recognition in his eyes when I spoke Michael Doyle's name, I knew that I had been right. Carl Bauer, as well as heaven knew how many others, had heard rumors of Amanda's conduct.

"Don't you see?" I asked. "You mustn't let him know, at least not tonight. He might rush up to Amanda's room in a rage—"

"And that would be very bad for her. Don't worry. I'll not tell Mr. Dorrance. And if later on he upbraids me for it, I'll remind him that my first duty was to my patient." He paused. "I've already told Amanda that if she wants to get in touch with me out here this weekend, or next week in New York, I'll do anything I can for her. Well, goodnight, Emma."

I waited until I was sure that he must have left the house. Then I went back to Amanda. She said, as I sat down by the bed, "He told you?"

"Yes. Does Michael know?"

She shook her head.

"Why not?"

"I didn't want to tell him until after we were married. I mean, I didn't want him to feel that we *had* to get married. I thought that if he could win Papa over tonight, we'd get married right away, and go off on a honeymoon. I even asked Michael to make reservations on the *Mauretania*. It's sailing for England next week. And later on we could say that the baby was premature."

I looked down at her white face with exasperation as well as pity. What a hopeless dreamer she was. After her recklessness of last summer, after all those hours she must have spent in the apartment of a man she knew

112

her father would not accept, she expected a prim and proper storybook outcome, complete with a paternal blessing.

I said, "Dr. Bauer isn't going to tell your father. But perhaps you should tell him tomorrow. He'll see that you and Michael simply must get married."

"But he won't! Now that I know what he's capable of—buying up all those debts of poor Mr. Doyle's, I mean—I know that he'll never give in. He'd just ship me off someplace until I had the baby."

Although I didn't say so, I also felt that he would do exactly that. After awhile I said, "But what do you intend to do?"

"I'll just wait. In spite of what he said about never seeing me again, Michael will get in touch with me somehow. Then we'll work something out." Her eyes closed. "I'd like to rest now."

13

Unable to sleep, I read until past three in the morning. Thus it was almost ten when I awoke. I dressed, went downstairs, and found the breakfast room blessedly empty. The maids, though, had left coffee for me, warmed by a spirit lamp, and breakfast rolls and fruit.

When I'd finished breakfast I went back upstairs. Just as I reached the landing Mrs. Dorrance emerged from Amanda's room. She closed the door behind her and then, wearing her remote smile, walked toward me. "Good morning, Emma."

"Good morning, Mrs. Dorrance. How is Amanda?"

"She says she's feeling much better this morning, but she does appear run-down, just as young Dr. Bauer said."

"You've seen him?"

"No. I took a sleeping draught soon after my dinner last night, and slept so soundly that I didn't even know Dr. Bauer had been here. But about an hour ago my husband came to my room and told me about it."

An hour ago, and she had gone to see Amanda only now.

I said, "I think I'll go in and see her, unless she told you she wanted to rest."

"She didn't."

When I entered her room I found Amanda lying, fully clothed, on the chaise longue. Although still pale, she seemed quite calm. After we had talked for a few minutes I said, "How about a walk down to the beach? It would do you good."

"Oh, no! I must stay here, so that when Michael tries to get in touch with me . . ."

Not if. When. "Amanda, how can he get in touch with you today? It's too soon for you to get a letter, even if he ran the risk of sending you one. And he's certainly not going to risk phoning. With several phones in this house, how could he be sure someone else was not listening?"

"Just the same, he'll get in touch. One of the servants will bring me a note, or something like that. I'm sure of it."

I gave up arguing with her. At her suggestion, we played Russian bank until, at one o'clock, Sara arrived with her tray. I went downstairs. I found only Mr. Dorrance and Larry at the luncheon table, eating in silence. Larry's white face had a look of rigid control. I helped myself to poached fish and salad. After I sat down I ventured to ask, "Is Lucy ill?"

"Thorsen has driven Lucy into New York," John Dorrance said, "where she'll catch the train for Boston. Until she enters college she'll be staying with the Hepworths."

I'd heard mention of the Hepworths, a family connection of the Dorrances.

I looked at John Dorrance with grudging admiration. Only last Thursday morning he had returned from Europe to find his family in what he considered appalling disarray. With fists flying, so to speak, he had attacked the situation. He had blocked that upstart Irishman out of his elder daughter's life. He had banished Lucy to Boston. And he had ordered Larry to a school he was sure to loathe. And all within a little more than forty-eight hours.

I said, "I suppose you'll be going in to your New York office on Monday."

"No. My office can run itself for a little while longer. That European trip took a lot out of me. I think I'll stay here for a while and enjoy the September weather. September's the best month in the Hamptons, you know."

I felt sure that his decision to linger in East Hampton had nothing to do with the weather. He wanted to keep Amanda out here, where it would be easier to make sure that she and Michael Doyle did not see each other.

"How about you, Emma? You can spend another couple of weeks with us, can't you?"

"No, Mr. Dorrance. I'm to have a position at the Bradley School when it opens on the twenty-first. I must go home on Monday to get ready."

"I'm sorry, and not just for Amanda's sake. I too enjoy having you here."

Not for the first time, I realized that John Dorrance liked me. I only wished that his behavior toward his children had not made it impossible for me to like him. "Thank you, Mr. Dorrance."

"And how about you, Larry?"

He raised his white, bitter face. "Sir?"

"You enjoy our having a young lady as our house guest, don't you? It's far more interesting than having just your sisters for company, isn't it?"

Larry said, pure hatred in his eyes, "Of course, sir."

After lunch I pedaled to the club. Leaving my bicycle in the club's rack, I wandered for at least two hours along the almost deserted beach. This was indeed the fine September weather Mr. Dorrance had mentioned. Sunlight ran like quicksilver along the blades of breeze-stirred dune grass. That same breeze blew foam back from the low rollers' crests, so that they suggested miniature white horses charging toward shore, manes streaming. In the northern part of the blue, blue sky a few fluffy little clouds floated, creating the impression that almost infinite distances stretched between me and the horizon. I walked slowly, stopping often to pick up and admire for a moment a scallop shell, or a bit of wood polished to a satin sheen by who could say how many years of salt air and sunlight. Several times I turned a horseshoe crab's discarded shell over with my foot. I had read somewhere that this species, predating the dinosaurs, had been in existence longer than almost any other form of crustacean. Even before I knew that, I had always found those big horseshoe crabs, with their whiplike tails and their shells like armor plate, both fascinating and a little frightening.

When the watch pinned to my blouse told me that it was almost three o'clock, I turned around and started back to the club, walking more briskly than before.

I saw no one as I entered the Dorrances' house and climbed the stairs to my room. But I had just finished changing clothes when Amanda knocked on my door.

"Emma, I've asked Sara to bring a dinner tray for you to my room tonight. Is that all right?"

"That's fine." In fact, I was glad that she had given me an excuse not to share another uncomfortable meal with John Dorrance and his son.

During our dinner in her room I finally asked her if she had received any sort of word from Michael.

"No, but I will tomorrow. I'm sure of it."

The next day, Sunday, she seemed far less confident. Even though she did not mention her pregnancy, I could see that she was becoming more and more frightened by the hour. In midmorning, at her request, I bicycled to the village and from one of its two public phones called the number she had given me, the number of Michael's apartment. Then I had to come back and report that there was no answer.

I had lunch with her in her room, and then read aloud from *Sister Carrie*, again not sure how much she actually heard. Sure that she would protest bitterly, I kept putting off the task of telling her that I intended to go to New York on Monday. But in the evening, after Sara had taken away our dinner trays, I could delay no longer.

"Amanda, I must go to New York tomorrow."

I had been prepared to add that much as I wanted to help her, I had to think of my own future. And besides, I had planned to say, what real help could I give her just by staying here? The only effective help for her situation would be to have her father change his mind. And as long as she refused to let her father know about her child, there was little chance of his reconsidering.

But I did not have to say any of those things. "You know I hate to have you go," she said. Then, eagerly: "But in New York you'll have a better chance of seeing Michael." A shadowed look crossed her face. "And if for some reason you don't find him right away, you can talk to his father and learn where he is. Then you can let me know."

"Oh, Amanda! How can I let you know without running the risk that—"

"We'll make up a code, a telephone code. I'll know what you're saying, but anyone listening in will think that we're just talking about clothes or something.

After a long moment I said reluctantly, "Well, we can try it."

14

I reached Brooklyn the next day in time for lunch. Of course I told my mother nothing of what had happened in East Hampton—nothing, at least, that would disturb her pride in the "fine" friends her daughter had made. I said merely that the weather had been wonderful, that Mr. Dorrance had come home from Europe looking well, and that I had bicycled, played tennis, and walked on the beach.

My mother told me that at two that afternoon she was going to a meeting of her chapter of the Brooklyn Garden Club.

"Mama, I've always wondered. Why should a garden club meet in September?"

"Why, to talk about potted plants, of course. More chocolate pudding, dear? Then I won't, either. I'd better get dressed."

At our house there was only one phone, in a cubbyhole under the stairs. As soon as my mother had gone to her room I went to the cubbyhole, lit its gas jet with a match from the box on the telephone table, and closed the door. Then I called Michael Doyle's number.

A man answered. Even though I was almost sure he was not Michael, I asked, "Is this Mr. Michael Doyle?"

"No, this is the apartment manager." In the background I could hear the loud voices of other men, and a scraping sound, as if furniture was being dragged across the floor. "Mr. Doyle gave up this apartment last Saturday."

"Gave it up! But where did he go?"

"I don't know. I only know that he left with two suitcases of personal belongings, and that this morning movers arrived to take his furniture to storage."

I thanked him and hung up. Then, after a moment, I lifted the telephone book from its shelf beneath the phone table and looked up Matthew Doyle's business number.

A woman, I suppose the operator of Matthew Doyle's private switchboard, put me through to a male employee, who told me that Mr. Doyle was "occupied" at the moment.

"Please," I said. "Tell him I'm calling about his son."

Within seconds a deep voice holding more than a trace of brogue said, "Matthew Doyle speaking."

"Mr. Doyle, this is Emma Hoffsteader. Has Michael mentioned me to you?"

"Yes. You're a friend of that Dorrance girl."

I wondered what John Dorrance would have thought if he had heard "the Irish saloonkeeper" refer to his daughter as "that Dorrance girl." He added, his voice more tense now, "What is this about my son?"

I heard footsteps in the hall above, moving toward the stairs. "Mr. Doyle, may I come to see you this afternoon?"

121

"How soon can you get here?"

"Perhaps in an hour."

"Two-thirty, then."

"About that. Goodbye, Mr. Doyle."

A little more than an hour later, Matthew Doyle seated me in his office. With its rolltop desk and plain wooden chairs, it reminded me of my father's office, except that on the walls, instead of prints of the Black Forest and Rhine castles, there were photographs of pugilists, wearing tights and with fists aggressively poised. Mr. Doyle himself, tall and silver-haired, was a handsome man. Perhaps in his youth he had been as good-looking as Michael.

He said, "All right, Miss Hoffsteader, about my son. Do you know where he is?"

I said, dismayed, "No, I hoped you did."

I could tell my answer was a blow to him. After a moment he said, "All I know is that he came to me late Saturday afternoon and said he was going away for a while. He wouldn't tell me where."

"Did he give you a reason for not telling you?"

"Yes!" Bitterness in the dark blue eyes that were so like Michael's. "Evidently that Dorrance girl had hurt him very much, although he wouldn't tell me how. He told me that he doesn't want to see her, ever again. And he figured that if I didn't know where he had gone, I couldn't tell her, no matter how much she wheedled."

I understood then. "Mr. Doyle, I'm afraid your son felt it necessary to deceive you. It's for your sake, not his, that he's broken with Amanda."

"My sake! Why, I never tried to separate the boy from

her. True, I thought it would be better for him to marry a nice Irish girl, not someone from a stuffed shirt—"

"Please, Mr. Doyle, let me explain," I said, and then stopped, not knowing how to go on. After perhaps half a minute I said, "Mr. Doyle, you—you owe quite a lot of money, don't you?"

He looked both surprised and indignant. "Miss Hoffsteader! What do my business affairs have to do with—"

"Please, Mr. Doyle. They have everything to do with your son. So—so please make this easier for me by answering."

After a moment he said, "All right! I've been expanding very fast, and to do it I've borrowed money from a number of sources."

"In the form of what business people call demand notes?"

He shot me a startled look. "Yes, in order to get the best terms. I haven't taken much of a risk. Oh, sure, if they all demanded their money at once . . . But that won't happen, not when my business is doing so well. Within a year I'll be able to pay them all off."

"But what if the money is demanded sooner?"

"Why should it be? The money is safe, and earning good interest."

"Just the same, what if it were demanded tomorrow?"

"Then everything would have to be sold to meet my obligations. I would be out on the street, bankrupt."

I told him, then, about that manila envelope in John Dorrance's study.

At last he said, white to the lips, "So that is how he forced my boy—Miss Hoffsteader, Michael loves that

123

girl very much. If I'd known the truth, I would have said let John Dorrance do his worst. What if he did break me? I could start over."

"You mean that, Mr. Doyle?"

"Of course I mean it!"

"Then when you hear from Michael, you'll tell him that. It's terribly important that he come back to Amanda. It's even more important than he knows."

Matthew Doyle looked at me for a long moment. At last he said softly, "So it is like that, is it? Oh, the poor girl. The poor mavourneen."

"But you have no idea where he has gone?"

He shook his head. "I just feel quite sure he is not in New York. Maybe he has gone somewhere in that little motor car he bought. Or maybe he went down to the docks and found a freighter that was shorthanded and shipped out on it. He did that one summer while he was still in college."

I sat in appalled silence. If he had left on a tramp steamer, it might be weeks before his father would receive a letter from him. At last I said, "Maybe he went somewhere on a passenger ship."

He shook his head. "The *Mauretania* sails later this week, but there have been no passenger ship sailings within the past few days. You see, lately I've bought bar concessions on two passenger lines, and I'm negotiating for more, and so I keep close track of arrivals and departures. But I'll make sure about it."

"And you'll let me know? We're the only Hoffsteaders in the Brooklyn phone book."

"Of course I will. And if it turns out that it is you that—that my boy gets in touch with—"

"I'll call you at once. Goodbye, Mr. Doyle."

When I reached home I was glad to find that my mother was still out. I went to the cubbyhole under the stairs and called the Dorrance's East Hampton number. Amanda must have been waiting right beside her phone, because it did not complete its first ring.

We exchanged how-are-you's. Then she asked, "Were you able to buy that knitting yarn I wanted?"

"No. I telephoned Altman's, but they don't have it. They have stopped—carrying it." I had told her, using the code we had devised the night before, that Michael was no longer at his apartment.

Her voice had a constricted sound. "And Lord and Taylor's?"

"I went there. The manager told me that he has no idea where I could find it."

I hoped she would understand from that that I had seen Michael's father in person, and that he had no idea where his son was. Evidently she did understand that, because when she spoke her voice was dull. "I see. Well, thank you, Emma. I had better hang up now. I want to wash my hair."

"But you'll call me?"

"Yes, of course. Goodbye, Emma."

For the next three days I heard nothing from her or about her. Despite my worry on her behalf, it was pleasant to have time to attend to my own concerns. I shopped for clothes, mostly serviceable skirts and shirt-waists which I thought would be suitable for the assistant to the headmistress of a girls' school. One afternoon I had tea with Miss Farnsworth. A tall, portly woman with rimless glasses perched on the bridge of her aquiline nose, she seemed to me much less awesome than she had when I was one of her pupils. By the time I left her flat I was feeling quite pleased by the prospect of working at the school.

That was on Wednesday. Past three o'clock the next day, John Dorrance phoned from East Hampton. Fortunately, my mother was out at the time. Since our cook was in the kitchen and both our housemaids somewhere upstairs, I answered the phone.

"Emma? This is John Dorrance."

I said, alarmed, "What's happened? Is Amanda—"

"She's not with you?"

"No!"

"She's disappeared. She must have left the house sometime in the very early morning and gone to the railroad station. Someone saw her get on the milk train." I knew, vaguely, that the train which carried dairy products to towns the length of Long Island left very early, perhaps as early as five in the morning.

He went on, "Emma, I hope you'll let me know as soon as she comes to you. She's bound to within the next few hours."

I was not at all sure of that. Because of her situation, she might very well hesitate to come here, lest something in her appearance or manner betray her to those two gentle but thoroughly respectable people who were my parents.

I said, "She may not come here."

"Of course she will! She's not at the Fifth Avenue house. I just called Mrs. Nesbitt. And so she's bound to come to you. Why shouldn't she?"

For several seconds I silently debated with myself.

Should I tell him why? Amanda had said it would be no use, that he would only "ship me off someplace" until she had the baby. But perhaps she was wrong. Certainly he sounded shaken now. If he knew the truth, he might soften toward Michael, and might use his considerable resources to find him.

I took the plunge. "I'll tell you why Amanda might not come here. She's going to have Michael Doyle's child. I think she would be afraid that my parents, or at least my mother, would suspect that."

What seemed a long time passed. Then he said, in an expressionless voice, "Will you please say that again?"

I said it.

"The slut," his voice was slow and even. "The unspeakable little slut. I've always loved her more than anyone or anything in the world, given her more—"

"Slut or not," I cried, "she needs you. She needs you first of all to help find Michael. He's gone, and we don't know where. And she needs you to forgive her, forgive them both, so they can be married—"

"I'll be goddamned if I will! Do you think I'm going to accept that Irishman's bastard as my grandson?"

Never before in talking to me had he used the mildest curse word. The violence of his language now told me just how enraged he was.

"She didn't consult me before she made her bed," he went on. "Now let her lie in it. And for all I care, she can lie in it alone for the rest of her life."

I said, after several seconds, "Surely you can't mean that. You can't just turn your back—"

"Oh, yes I can. Not that I won't give her money, quite a generous amount of money, to pay her for staying away from the rest of us. Ten thousand dollars, in fact. As soon as you hear from her—" He broke off. "Or perhaps you have some idea of where she has gone."

"Yes, I have an idea."

I thought he might question me on that point, but he did not. "Very well. As soon as you've talked to her, let me know. I'll send a check to whatever address she cares to use. But that will be it. When that money is gone, she'll get no more out of me. Is that clear?"

"Completely clear."

But I did not believe him. Oh, I could understand his fury. Amanda had outraged him in almost every possible way. She had defied his parental authority, and thrown his proud affection back in his face. By falling in love with what many would consider her social inferior, she had flouted the class in which she had been raised. And she had flouted the double moral standard which, while permitting sexual license to him, denied it to his daughter.

But later, surely, he would reconsider. He would start thinking about Amanda as a tiny infant, and on a pony at six, and dressed for dancing school at eight. And he would start realizing that the child would be, not just "that Irishman's bastard," but Amanda's son or daughter. And then he would use his considerable powers to set things right.

I only hoped that by then it would not be too late.

"All right, Mr. Dorrance. Goodbye."

15

After I hung up I told myself that it was too late in the day for me to go to Rose Shannon's place. But the truth was that no matter at what hour John Dorrance's call had come, I would have wanted to put off returning to that bleak railroad flat and the woman who had given birth to Amanda.

Early the next afternoon, though, I knocked on Rose Shannon's door. When she opened it I could tell she was not surprised to see me.

"Come in, Miss Hoffsteader."

"Emma," I said, moving past her into the room. A nervous smile on her face, she closed the door.

"All right, Emma."

Her hair was combed today, and she wore, not the soiled yellow kimona, but a white shirtwaist and a gray skirt. What was more, she appeared completely sober. The same could not be said of Hank Dunkerly. He sat, glass in hand, on a straight chair with its back tilted against the wall. Even from several feet away I could smell alcohol.

Smiling, he lifted his glass in salute. "Hello there, Miss

Hoffmeyer or whatever your name is. Nice to see you again."

Rose Shannon said, "Hank, didn't you say you had to go someplace?"

"Me? Of course not. Where are your manners, Rosie? Ask the young lady to sit down."

For a moment Rose Shannon looked at him with baffled eyes. Then she gestured toward the armchair. I sat down, and she sat facing me on the battered sofa.

"Offer her a drink, Rosie."

I said, before she could speak, "No, thank you." Then, because I was sure that her "fiancé, sort of," would not leave until he was good and ready to, I decided to bring up the subject of her daughter immediately.

"Mrs. Shannon, has Amanda been to see you?"

"Yes, she came yesterday. And she's still here."

"Here?" My gaze went to the doorway that led to the kitchen and to the bedroom beyond.

"I meant here in the building. You see, there were a couple of vacant flats, both furnished. She took the one on the second floor."

"Right below this one," Hank Dunkerly said. "I was down there about half an hour ago. Moved the icebox so she could clean behind it. Lots of roaches back there, of course." He laughed. "She didn't scream or anything, but from the look on her face I'd say she never seen a cockroach before." He took a swallow of his drink and then said, "How come John Dorrance's daughter is in a dump like this? Oh, I know she was Rosie's kid. But still, how come?"

"Hank!"

Ignoring her, he still looked at me. "The girl's in a jam, huh? Does Dorrance know?"

"Hank!" Rose Shannon sprang to her feet. "Now you get out of here! I mean it. Get out."

He laughed. Nevertheless, he got to his feet and placed his empty glass on the mantel. "All right, ladies. I was going to leave anyway. An old carny pal of mine's in town. Think I'll mosey over to this hangout of his on Third Avenue."

When the door had closed behind him, Rose sank back onto the sofa. After a moment I asked, "Did Amanda tell you about the trouble she's in?"

Rose nodded. "All of it."

"How does she seem?"

"I don't know. Funny. Hysterical, I guess you'd say. One minute talking about how everything's going to be all right, how she's going to hire detectives to find this Michael, and the next minute crying." She paused. "Do you have any idea where Michael might be?"

"No. His father thinks he may just have gone down to the docks and signed onto some freighter that was about to leave port, some ship that was short-handed."

"If he did, it might be weeks or even months before—"

I nodded.

"Emma, she mustn't stay here. This place is no good for her. *I'm* no good for her. I—I drink. I haven't had a drop since she came here yesterday afternoon, but I'll start again, and then what good will I be to her? I won't even be able to protect her from Hank."

She drew a deep breath. "He's the main reason I want her to leave. Oh, he'd say it's just because I'm jealous, but of course it's not just that. Emma, he's dangerous in more ways than one. Last night he was really drunk. Usually he just stays sort of mellow. But last night he really tied one on. And he said to me, 'I wonder how much a rag like the *Clarion-Telegraph* would pay me if I tipped them off about you and Dorrance and his daughter? Why, they might pay enough to set me up in the carny business again.'

"So if you could persuade her to go home . . . If she tells her father the trouble she's in, I'm sure he'll stand by her. I mean, I know he can be a pretty cold, hard man. All these years he's just sent money, never once looked me up to find out how I was getting along. Still, I'm sure he'd stand by Amanda."

"No."

"What do you mean, no?"

"He won't stand by her. He knows the truth. And he says he never wants to see her again."

I told her then about my telephone conversation with John Dorrance the previous afternoon.

For a moment there was despair in her face. Then she rallied. "What you told him must have knocked him for a loop. Maybe that's why he said what he did. But maybe after he calms down . . ."

"Yes, that occurred to me too." I stood up. "I'll go see her now. Perhaps she and I can work something out. At least I can tell her that she won't have to stay here, not after her father sends her the ten thousand."

She brightened. "That's right. And as long as Hank don't learn she's getting all that money— You'll warn her about that, won't you?"

I nodded.

"She's in Two-C, right below this flat."

In the second floor corridor I knocked on the door of 2-C. Amanda called in a voice so dull I scarcely recognized it, "Come in."

The front room here, like the one in the flat above, had a window opening on the narrow space between this building and the next. Since it was on a lower floor, perhaps her flat was even darker than her mother's. Anyway, she'd lit the gas jet. She sat in a rocking chair directly beneath where the gas fixture jutted out of the wall. Beside her on the floor lay a broom.

The sight of her was such a shock that for a moment I stood riveted. Right then she bore a striking resemblance to her mother, or perhaps to her own self a decade or so in the future. As Rose Shannon had the first time I saw her, she wore a kimona, not a yellow one, but a lovely turquoise one I had seen many times before. There was a smear of grease on one sleeve, probably the result of her labors in the kitchen. Her hair was disordered, and had lost its lovely sheen.

She said, "Hello, Emma. I was trying to clean up a little, but I got tired—" She broke off, and then added, "How did you know I was here?"

"I guessed."

For the moment she just accepted that. "Well, welcome to the Ritz. And sit down."

I sat down in a brown mohair armchair and then threw an appalled look around me. Someone a long time ago had made the worst possible color choice for a room filled with perpetual twilight. The wallpaper was brown, with squares and rectangles of lighter brown where pictures had once hung. The carpet, threadbare in spots, was brown, and so was the sagging-springed sofa.

Amanda said, "How did you know I'd left East Hampton? Did you try to phone me?"

"No. Your father phoned me."

She said bitingly, "Think of that! Maybe he really cares."

"Amanda, I meant well. But I'm afraid I made a terrible mistake."

She cocked her head to one side. "What did you do? Tell him I'm going to have Michael's baby?" I nodded. "And what did he say?"

"That he never wants to see you again."

She said, with bleak triumph, "Isn't that exactly what I told you he'd say if he knew? And don't worry about having made a mistake. If I'd stayed there, sooner or later he would have found out anyway."

"He says he'll send you a check for ten thousand dollars. He'll send it to any address you give me."

"If he sends me a check, I'll tear it up."

"Amanda! Don't be an idiot. How are you going to get along without money? How much have you got right now, by the way?"

"The rent was ten dollars a month, in advance. I guess I've got about twenty dollars."

"Amanda, if you don't take your father's money—"

"I told you I won't! After what he did to Michael, after what he's done to both Michael and me, I wouldn't touch a cent of his, even if I were starving."

I recalled that her father told her that people who had never lacked for money were the ones who failed to realize how important it was. He had been right about that.

"Your twenty dollars will be gone soon. What then?"

"Rose Shan— My mother will stand by me."

I tried to speak gently. "She thinks you should leave."

"I know. She's afraid that awful Dunkerly person— But he won't. I slapped his face when he was down here about an hour ago. He just laughed and said, 'Okay. You can't blame a fellow for trying, but it won't happen again.'"

"Maybe it won't. But even so, this horrible place— Please, Amanda. Telephone your father. Plead with him."

She stared at me. "Emma, are you out of your head? I just told you that I won't touch a cent of his money. And yet you think I might grovel to him."

I said, after a long silence, "Then come home to Brooklyn with me. You must have brought a suitcase. Pack it, and we'll leave."

"Oh, Emma. You think I'm going to inflict myself on those two darling people? I know how much you love your mother and father. That would be a terrible way to repay you for your friendship."

I hoped she did not see my relief.

Looking down at the floor, I reflected that there was one thing I could do. Since she would not plead with her father, I would have to plead for her. And I would do it face to face.

I stood up. With none of the litheness she used to have, she got up from the rocker. "Amanda, I'll go now. But I'll be back soon. And in the meantime, if you need me—"

"I know. I'll telephone you. There is a public phone in the bakery on the corner." She threw her arms around my neck and kissed my cheek. "Goodbye, Emma darling."

When I entered our Brooklyn house I heard my mother's voice, singing a scale to a piano accompaniment, from behind the parlor's closed double door. Sensible and thrifty in all other respects, my mother had one little vanity. For years she had taken lessons in hope of improving her contralto enough that she would be asked to sing before the Lieder Society.

I went directly to the cubbyhole under the stairs and called the Dorrances' East Hampton number. Edith answered, and immediately recognized my voice. "Oh, yes, Miss Emma. He's here, in his study. I'll tell him it's you calling."

Seconds later I heard John Dorrance say, "Hello, Emma."

"Mr. Dorrance, I've seen Amanda."

"Yes." Not even, where did you see her. Just yes.

"Let me come and talk to you about her."

"There's no necessity for that. Just tell me where to send the check."

"She says she doesn't want money."

"She'll change her mind about that. Not even Amanda can be that headstrong and foolish, not indefinitely."

"Please let me come to see you."

"If you intend to get me to change my mind, and I'm sure you do, you'll just be wasting your time."

"Please see me, anyway."

"All right. I'll be in town next week. Come to my office."

"I don't feel that I should wait until next week. Can't I come out to East Hampton tomorrow?"

"All right, Emma. Come ahead, as long as you realize I haven't changed my mind. No matter what Amanda has done, I'm always glad to see you."

"Thank you. I'll be there on the early afternoon train."

16

Thorsen met me at the station the next afternoon. It was one of those windy days that often occur near the time of the autumnal equinox. A double page of newsprint blew along the station platform. On the opposite side of the street the leaves and branchlets of elm trees moved as if stirred by the current of an invisible river.

As Thorsen carried my valise along the platform toward the Pierce-Arrow, I asked, "How is the family?"

"I really couldn't say, miss." So friendly toward me in the past, he now spoke with a cool politeness. "Mr. Dorrance is the only one still in East Hampton."

"Really? I knew Miss Lucy had gone to Boston. But have Mrs. Dorrance and Mr. Lawrence left too?"

"They went to New York two days ago."

"So soon?"

"They are to order uniforms for Mr. Lawrence at Brooks Brothers, I believe."

Uniforms for poor Larry to wear at the Virginia Military Institute.

We had reached the Pierce-Arrow. Thorsen put my

valise beside the driver's seat and then opened the rear door for me. When I was seated in the car he said, hand on the door, "As for Miss Amanda, she is still in New York, as you probably know."

He closed the door. So that was the reason he had turned unfriendly. He knew at least something of Amanda's situation. And he felt that I must have abetted her in her immoral folly. Perhaps in a way I had. Perhaps I should have tried to bring myself to write to her father in Europe about her conduct, or to tell Clara Dorrance. But both Amanda and I were young. And the young seldom betray each other to the older generation.

Thorsen had closed the glass panel between his compartment and mine. We rode in silence to the Dorrance house, where he stopped the car at the foot of the steps. Still silent, he climbed the steps beside me, carrying my valise.

John Dorrance must have been watching my arrival, because he himself opened the front door and took the valise from Thorsen's hand. "Hello, Emma." He closed the door and set down the valise. "One of the maids will take your valise up. Now how about some refreshment? Sara just bought a pot of coffee to the study."

A moment or so later, in the study, I saw that now the autumn crocuses definitely were in bloom. A bouquet of purple ones in a blue glass vase stood on the desk, along with a silver tray holding a coffeepot and two cups. I wondered if he remembered that it was to look at the autumn crocuses that we had gone back to the garden beyond the reflecting pool, that day when he flew into such a rage at his son.

When we were seated on opposite sides of the desk, coffee cups in hand, he said with a grim little smile, "All right, Emma, let's get it out of the way. Speak your little piece."

I tried the approach I had decided upon during that long train ride out from the city. "Do you know where Amanda is?"

"I assume she is somewhere in New York."

"She rented a ten-dollar-a-month flat in the house where Rose Shannon lives, on West Eighteenth Street."

He set down his cup in its saucer, hard. Blood rushed into his face and then ebbed, leaving him paler than before. But when he spoke his voice was even. "How did that happen?"

I told him about Amanda's hiring the detective to find out about her natural mother.

"She spent a busy summer, didn't she?" Now he could not keep the enraged tremble out of his voice.

"Perhaps she should not have done it without consulting you and Mrs. Dorrance," I admitted. "But that doesn't alter the fact that now she is in a dreadful, sunless flat, with only about twenty dollars in—"

"She won't stay there, once she gets my check. She'll use the money, for all her brave talk."

I was not in the least sure of that. He went on, "You think I'm a hard, cruel man, don't you? Did you ever consider that a hard man would not have adopted Amanda in the first place? After all, I had a legitimte child on the way—two of them, as it turned out. And I wasn't impelled by any overwhelming emotion for her mother. What feeling I'd had for her, and it had never been much, had disappeared. Just the same, I felt honor bound to adopt the child, and save her from the kind of life she'd have had if she'd been raised by Rose Shannon."

He paused for a moment. "When she was still only a few weeks old, I began to love her as I've never loved my other two children. I gave her everything I could. She threw it all in my face. And now she's back where she would have been if I'd ignored her existence nineteen years ago. She's with Rose Shannon, and *like* Rose Shannon."

He stopped speaking. After a moment I said, into the silence, "She went to Rose Shannon because she felt she had no one else. No one older than herself, anyway."

"Give it up, Emma! You're not going to make me feel guilty, and you're not going to get me to change my mind. If you want to help Amanda, tell her to bank that check as soon as she gets it. I'll send it to the box number I've been sending Rose Shannon's money to all these years. Ten thousand dollars ought to last even someone as reckless as Amanda for a long time.

"And now let's forget it. When are you going back to town?"

I said heavily, "I suppose on tomorrow morning's train."

"Stay longer, if you like."

"No, thank you. I have things I must do in town."

"Well, I'm sorry it is such a windy day. Otherwise you could enjoy the garden, or walk down to the beach for the sunset. But at least I can promise you a good dinner. And afterward, if you like, we will play chess."

It was an excellent dinner, with roast Long Island duckling as its main course. Throughout the meal John

141

Dorrance talked of his travels in Europe that summer. I sensed that he was trying to both charm and entertain, almost as if I had been, not a plain girl of less than twenty, but an attractive woman in her thirties, or perhaps a business acquaintance whose good will he needed. In short, I felt he was trying to make me like him, in spite of his attitude toward Amanda. And that, I told myself, meant that he did feel somewhat guilty, despite his protestations to the contrary.

After dinner, we played chess in front of the fire he had lighted in the library. I became even more sure that he was uneasy in his mind. On the few former occasions when we'd played, he had won without too much trouble. But that night he lost his queen on his tenth move, and resigned.

I went upstairs to bed. The wind was even stronger now, making the catalpa tree outside my window creak, and whistling around the corner of the house in a way I remembered from previous windy nights I had spent in this room. Despite the noisy wind and my unhappy thoughts, I finally slept, only to come awake in the darkness with a sense of loud voices somewhere on the ground floor of the house. For a moment or two the impression persisted. Then I could hear only the wind. It had been a dream, I concluded, a dream in which I had been reliving the night a furious and despairing Michael Doyle had fled from this house. I went back to sleep.

This time it was a crash that awoke me, a crash so loud that it could not have been part of a dream. I sat bolt upright in the dawn grayness.

The wind was noisier than ever. Through the creak of

tree branches and that eerie whistling around the corner of the house, I heard another sound from downstairs, a banging noise, as if the front door had been blown open and was now slamming against the wall. Knowing that I could not get back to sleep until I investigated, I put on my robe and left the room.

At the head of the stairs I looked down and saw that I had been right. The front door was open and had swung back against the wall. Fragments of a tall Chinese urn that had always stood near the doorway lay scattered over the parquet floor. Doubtless the vase had been toppled by the same gust of wind that had blown the door open. Wondering why the door had not been bolted, as usual, from the inside, I descended the stairs to close it.

I had almost reached it when something made me stop and look to my right. The door of the study stood open. Beyond it lamplight mingled with the dawn grayness.

Feeling weighted with a nameless premonition, I walked to the study and stood rooted in its doorway.

John Dorrance lay face down in front of his open safe. The back of his gray cardigan sweater—a sweater he must have put on after I went upstairs, because he had not been wearing it during our chess game—was soaked with blood. I did not know then that the blood was from multiple stab wounds. I only knew that there was a lot of it, so much that I could tell only by the sweater's sleeves that its color was gray. The weapon which had wreaked all that havoc, that ivory-handled letter opener, was still in his back.

For a few moments I had a blessed sense of unreality.

143

As if in a dream I looked at the still figure and the green-shaded electric lamp on the desk and the vase of crocuses. Then I thought, why, someone has killed him. He had to be dead, after losing all that blood. I saw now that there was also blood on the worn, rose-colored Kerman rug on which he lay.

And yet I still could not believe he was dead. How was it that John Dorrance, with all his power and ability and passion, could end like that, an inert figure in a blood-soaked sweater?

Don't faint, I ordered myself. Reach out your hand and pick up the telephone. Ask the operator to connect you with the police.

I took a step forward. Then I halted. A small object lay on the carpet, a few inches from John Dorrance's pale, oustretched right hand. I moved toward it, bent, picked it up.

One half of a gold cuff link, initialed M.T.D.

Michael Doyle there on the bench in the starlight, sun-browned hands clasped around his right knee, gold cuff link gleaming faintly as he talked of an Irish village called Loughglen—

So he had come back here last night. Again he had quarreled with Amanda's father, so loudly that I had heard it even through the wind's uproar. And then—

I laid the cuff link on the desk and stared down at it. Should I get rid of it? Oh, how I wanted to! But a life had been taken. Could I bring myself to—

Then I heard a sound almost beside me, a kind of strangled scream, and knew that it was too late for me to get rid of that cuff link, even if I had decided to do so.

I turned. Edith stood there in a gray bathrobe,

middle-aged face crumpled with sleep, metal curlers showing through the ruffled white muslin cap she wore. Her sick gaze was fixed on John Dorrance. She gave a little whimper and said, "Oh, Miss Emma! I heard this crash and—Who did it to him, who did it?"

Instead of answering I said, "I was about to telephone the police."

She looked at the telephone and then said, "What's that?" Stepping past me, she picked up the cuff link and held it on her palm. "M.T.D."

Her eyes lifted to mine, and I knew that she too was remembering that night when Michael Doyle had yelled up the stairs, "We can't see each other again. And if you want to know why, ask your son of a bitch of a father."

Edith said, "So he came back and—"

"Please give it to me."

She handed me the cuff link. Stomach churning, I placed it where I had found it, just beyond that still, outstretched hand. Then I turned to the telephone.

17

Almost thirty hours later I sat on a New York–bound train.

Throughout those thirty hours the shock of finding John Dorrance's body had persisted, so that for me everything had an odd, unreal quality. I could not even have said how long it was after I called them that the East Hampton constable and his deputy arrived, nor am I sure just what questions the constable put to the servants and me after he had gathered us all in the library. I do know that he was still questioning us when the police from the county seat at Riverhead—two uniformed men and a Dr. Somebody-or-other and a Sergeant McNamara in civilian clothes—reached the house. But I'm not sure how much later on it was that Sergeant McNamara called me back into the library alone for questioning. It must have been before noon, though, because I can recall sunlight slanting through an eastern window onto one sleeve of his brown jacket and onto the side of his middle-aged face with its bushy blond mustache. By that time my sense of shock, while still there, had worn off enough that his questions and my answers remained fairly clear in my memory.

He said, glancing into a small black leather notebook, "You told the constable that you picked up an initialed cuff link from the carpet."

"Yes, but I put it back just where it had been."

"You knew who it belonged to?"

I said wretchedly, "As I told the constable—or at least I think I told him—I'm sure it must be Michael Doyle's. His middle name is Terence. Besides, I think he was wearing gold oval cuff links when he came to a party in this house last June."

"And of course he is the same Michael Doyle you and the servants mentioned to the constable, the one who quarreled violently with Mr. Dorrance about ten days ago."

"Yes."

"Over Mr. Doyle's attentions to Mr. Dorrance's daughter, as I understand it."

"That's—that's not the way it was! They love each other very much, and they wanted to marry. Mr. Dorrance not only forbade it. He threatened financial reprisals against Michael's father."

"You told the constable that you have no idea where Michael Doyle is."

"I don't. Neither does his father. He told me about a week ago that he thinks his son might have shipped out on some freighter."

"It appears that he did not. Instead he came here last night and had a ruckus with Mr. Dorrance. Apparently it turned into a physical struggle, in the course of which the young man lost half a cuff link. We haven't found the other half, although it may be somewhere on the driveway. We figure it must have stayed in his cuff until after he bolted from the house, leaving the door so insecurely closed that some time later a blast of wind blew it open."

He paused and then said, "But before he left he drove that letter opener several times into Mr. Dorrance's back."

I cried, sickened, "You can't be sure of that!"

"No, but that's the way it looks, doesn't it?" When I remained silent he went on, "I understand that Miss Amanda Dorrance has left her family. Do you know where she is?"

He'd find out sooner or later. I gave him the West Eighteenth Street address.

"Now to get back to Mr. Dorrance. It appears that he died several hours before you found him. During the night did you hear anything unusual from downstairs, like the sound of a quarrel?"

"Once I thought I did, but it might have been just wind sounds." I paused. "Maybe someone else heard quarreling."

"No. In fact, the only one besides yourself who even realized that the door must have blown open was that housemaid, Evelyn West."

"Edith West."

He glanced into his notebook. "That's right, Edith West. Sara Murphy, the other housemaid who remained here after Mrs. Dorrance took several servants to New York with her, says she heard nothing either last night or around dawn this morning, even though her third-floor room is next to Edith's. That gardener, Thorsen, says he heard nothing, which isn't surprising, since his cottage is two hundred yards behind the house. The cook, who was in her room next to the kitchen, heard the door banging, but thought it was a loose shutter on the third floor." He paused. "Now about that safe."

I nodded, remembering the safe's open door.

"Do you know how much money, if any, Mr. Dorrance had in it?"

"I'd have no way of knowing." I felt sudden hope. "You mean he was robbed?"

"Perhaps. The safe was empty except for some legal papers."

I cried, "If the man who did this was a thief, he couldn't have been Michael. Michael would have no reason to steal."

"Not unless he decided, after he'd killed Mr. Dorrance, to try to make the police think it had been done by an ordinary thief."

For a while I sat there in wretched silence. Then I said, "Weren't there fingerprints? I mean, I know that if there'd been one on the cuff link, I spoiled it by—"

"Don't feel guilty about that. Because of those engraved initials, the cuff link would not have taken a print anyway. The same goes for the handle of the letter opener. Too much carving on it. As for the safe, it was wiped clean. Until the fingerprint man finishes his examination of the room, we won't know whether or not there were any prints there that don't belong to members of the household."

Hoping desperately that there was someone with

evidence that it had not been Michael in the study the night before, I said, "There is a three-man, twenty-four-hour patrol of Goddard Lane at this time of year. The four-to-midnight man is Orren Creavey. Did you ask—"

"Yes. Both the watchman on the four-to-midnight shift and the one on the midnight-to-eight shift have been questioned. Neither of them saw or heard anything, but then, neither of them would have been likely to unless he happened to be close when the fellow climbed over the wall."

"The wall?"

"Yes. The gates were locked, so whoever killed Mr. Dorrance probably climbed the wall. However, that would be no great trick. It's only seven feet high and made of rough stone, affording hand and footholds." He paused. "Well, I think that's all for now."

"Then may I go? To New York, I mean? There's an early afternoon train."

"We'd much rather you stayed here until tomorrow, just in case we need more information from you."

"Very well, but I'll go to my room now, if I may."

"Of course."

I started toward the door and then turned back. "Is Mrs. Dorrance on her way out from New York?"

"Not yet. She's been notified, of course. She said she would come out on the afternoon train rather than the morning one, so that she can wait in New York for her son."

"Wait for him? Isn't he with her?"

"No. It seems he went to Boston two days ago, but he's expected back in New York around noon today."

So he'd gone to say goodbye to his sister before being

shipped off to V.M.I. with his Brooks Brothers uniforms. Well, he wouldn't be needing those uniforms now.

I went out into the hall. As I passed the study's closed door I was thankful that at least John Dorrance no longer lay behind it. Sometime during that nightmarish morning a horse-drawn ambulance had arrived. Men had carried a laden stretcher from the house to the ambulance and then driven away.

Because I wanted my mother to hear from me what had happened, rather than from newsboys bawling a headline, I called her from the telephone on a table near the foot of the stairs. With difficulty I managed to soothe her semi-hysteria, and to convince her that I was perfectly safe and would be home the next day.

I went up to my room. With no appetite for lunch, I stayed there all that strangely unreal day, sometimes trying to read, but most of the time just staring out the window at the reflecting pool and the lines of rose bushes, some of them already wrapped in burlap against the coming winter.

It was getting dark when someone knocked. I opened the door. Mrs. Dorrance stood there in a smart, narrow-skirted green suit trimmed with black braid. Her black toque was trimmed with a bird's wing dyed green.

"Hello, Emma. No, I won't come in. I'm going to my room to take off my hat. Will you please come there in about ten minutes?"

By the time she admitted me to her sitting room ten minutes later she had not only removed her hat but had changed to a brown silk dress. She gestured me to a chair and then sat down on the small sofa.

I had been prepared to express some sort of condolences, but the words remained unspoken. I saw absolutely no sign of grief in her face. In a way, I respected her for not feigning an emotion she did not feel.

And so my first words were, "I suppose you have not talked to the police yet."

"But we have. A Sergeant McNamara was waiting for Larry and me on the station platform. He rode here with us in the Pierce-Arrow, and asked questions on the way. He's gone now but he said he was coming back tomorrow. In the meantime he's left a policeman down in the hall. Whether he's there to protect us or to keep us from running away, I couldn't say."

After a moment she went on, "Neither Larry nor I could tell him much about Michael Doyle beyond what you had told him."

When I made no response to that, she said, "Incidentally, Emma, if you're wondering if I know about Amanda's condition, I do. My husband told me. I was not in the least surprised. It is a classic case of like mother, like daughter."

I said nothing. After a while she went on, "When my husband told me that Amanda was pregnant, he did not know yet where she had gone. Do you know?"

"She's with her mother," I said evenly. "Or rather, she's taken a flat one floor below that of her mother."

"Then you've met Rose Shannon?" As I hesitated, she went on, "Oh, yes, Emma. I knew that Amanda was the child of my husband and a woman named Rose Shannon. For a while I accepted his story—and that of the lawyer we had then—that Amanda was the illegitimate offspring of some completely strange woman. Then I began to suspect the truth, and I made it my business to verify it."

I saw no reason to reply to that either. She asked, "Do you plan to see Amanda soon?"

"As soon as possible."

"She will be glad to hear that her father did not disinherit her. He intended to. When I called our lawyer today, he said that John had told him that as soon as he got back to town he intended to draw up a new will, disinheriting both Amanda and Larry. But of course now . . ."

Her voice trailed off. After a moment she added, "Well, I just wanted to learn if you knew where Amanda had gone."

Taking that as dismissal, I got to my feet. Then I said reluctantly, "One thing more. If you need help with the funeral arrangements . . ."

"Thank you, Emma. But I have already made the arrangements. The funeral will be strictly private, with only family members present, and it will be out here." She added, "I'll see you at dinner, although with the servants so upset we may not get dinner until all hours."

It was past eight-thirty when the dinner gong sounded. That meal was the most uncomfortable I had ever experienced. Larry, looking pale and withdrawn, said good evening to me and then did not speak again. For a few minutes Mrs. Dorrance and I kept up a stilted conversation about how much less crowded the trains were now that the summer was over. Then we too lapsed into silence.

At nine-thirty I went to my room. I had expected to lie awake, but my broken sleep of the night before,

153

followed by the strain of the long, long day, had exhausted me so much that I fell asleep almost immediately.

In the morning Sergeant McNamara arrived around nine o'clock. It would be all right, he said, for me to go to New York. I caught the one o'clock train.

It was running beneath the East River now. I stood up and took my valise down from the rack. In Penn Station I called my mother, saying that I would be home in an hour or so. Then I took a hansom cab to West Eighteenth Street.

I knocked on Amanda's door, waited, knocked again. No response. Anxiously I climbed the next flight of stairs and knocked on Rose Shannon's door. She opened it immediately. Over her shirtwaist and skirt she wore a green knitted shawl. On her dark head was a black straw hat trimmed with a somewhat bedraggled wreath of artificial daisies.

"Oh!" she said. "Come in. I was just about to go down to the corner and try to telephone you at your house in Brooklyn."

I said, moving past her, "Something's happened to Amanda, hasn't it?"

"Yes, she's in Bellevue. She's going to be all right, but she—she lost the baby last night."

I thought, perhaps it is just as well. But Amanda, I feared, was not feeling that way about it. "How did it happen?"

"She heard the newsboys in the street. There was an extra out about John being killed. She started running down the stairs, and tripped and fell. I—I had to leave

154

her in the downstairs hall while I ran to the bakery and got them to call an ambulance for me."

I thought of her lying in that dingy hallway, alone and grief-stricken and in pain—

"Couldn't Mr. Dunkerly have called the ambulance for you?"

Her face hardened. "That one! He wasn't here then. And this morning he left for good. I heard him moving around upstairs, so I went up there, and found him packing a suitcase. He said he was going upstate to work out some kind of a carny deal. I got the feeling he hadn't even intended to say goodbye to me."

I laid a sympathetic hand on her arm for a moment. Then I said, "I'm going to the hospital now."

Cabs were few in that neighborhood. I carried my valise clear across town, only dimly aware of the people I passed, and of the wagons and occasional motor truck clogging the street, and of the tired, end-of-summer look of the leaves on the trees lining the curb. In one of Bellevue's gloomy gray buildings a middle-aged nurse behind a desk said, "Amanda Dorrance? Go to Ward Twenty-three. That's two flights up."

There were eight other women in Amanda's ward. Eyes closed, she lay in the bed nearest the door. As I drew a straight chair from the wall and placed it beside her, the great violet eyes opened. "Hello, Emma." Her voice was almost toneless.

I sat down. "How are you feeling?"

"All right. I mean, I don't have any pain. Not now."

"Amanda, I'm so terribly sorry."

She nodded.

155

"I—I had to give the police that West Eighteenth Street address. Have they been to see you?"

"A police detective was here at the hospital this morning. He said the Suffolk County police had asked him to question me. I told him I had no idea where Michael is."

Her face twisted. "He didn't do it, Emma! You know Michael. You know he couldn't have. And—and if he had, in a rage, done a terrible thing like that, he wouldn't have run away afterward."

I thought, but whoever did do it ran away afterward. And there was that cuff link . . .

She said, "You're thinking about that cuff link they found, aren't you? It wasn't Michael's. Why, I'll bet there are thousands and thousands of men with those initials."

I did not point out how unlikely it was that a second man with those initials would have had reason to kill John Dorrance.

She closed her eyes. After a while tears seeped from under her eyelids and rolled down her cheeks. When she again spoke it was not of Michael.

"I came to hate him this past summer. But all the years before that I was so proud of him, and I loved him so much."

"I know." How could she not have felt that way about the handsome, powerful man who had praised and pampered her for nineteen years? After a moment I added, "I'm going to get you into another hospital."

"This one's all right."

"But you can afford the best. I know you're not

thinking about such matters now, but you have inherited a lot of money."

She said listlessly, "This hospital's still all right. Anyway, they tell me I won't be here for more than a week."

I saw no point in arguing with her. "I must go now, but I'll be back tomorrow."

"Thank you, Emma." For the first time she smiled. "Thank you for everything. It's so good to know that I haven't lost you too."

I thought of how much she had lost in only a few days. Her lover, her father, and now her unborn child. "I'll be back tomorrow," I repeated. "Goodbye, Amanda."

Even though it was almost six I still did not go immediately to Brooklyn. Instead, from a public phone in the hospital waiting room, I called the Manhattan number listed for both Dr. Carl Bauer's residence and office. Dr. Bauer himself answered the phone.

When I had finished telling him about Amanda's miscarriage he said, "Oh, that poor girl, that poor, foolish girl." I could imagine the sympathy in his big, gentle face.

"You must get her out of that awful hospital!"

"Now, Emma! People think of Bellevue in such terms only because it is free. The medicine practiced there is as good as any in the city, and better than that in a number of fancy private hospitals."

"I don't care! She's in a ward with eight other patients."

"All right, I'll see her tomorrow morning and offer to

arrange to put her in a semiprivate room. If she's depressed, and I don't see how she could help but be, it would not be wise for her to be all alone in a room. And after she's released from the hospital, I imagine it would be wise for her to go to a private sanitarium for a while. When I last saw her she looked very run-down. I know an excellent sanitarium in the Bronx."

"Thank you," I said. I left the hospital and hurried home to Brooklyn.

18

My name, of course had figured in the newspaper accounts of the John Dorrance case. I had feared that might lead the Bradley School to change its mind about hiring me as an assistant to the headmistress. It did not, however.

I found I enjoyed my work, even though I soon learned that secretary would have been a more suitable term for my position than assistant. I spent most of my days answering the telephone and writing letters for Miss Farnsworth in the elegant script I had learned at Bradley's. Typed letters, Miss Farnsworth felt, did not match the "tone" of a school such as hers.

I had been at work less than a week when, late one afternoon, a New York City detective called upon me at my parents' house. He was a youngish man, with a plain but surprisingly pleasant face. We talked in the side parlor, with the portrait of my mother's father, a Bavarian wine merchant, looking sternly down at us from a heavily bewhiskered face. The detective, I soon learned, was the same one who had come to the hospital to see Amanda the day after her father's death.

He said, "We've been wondering, Miss Hoffsteader, if you have remembered anything that might help us to find Michael Doyle."

"I haven't. Have you asked Miss Dorrance? She was transferred yesterday from Bellevue Hospital to Rosehill Sanitarium in the Bronx, you know."

"Yes, we know. In fact, I talked to her up there yesterday afternoon. She said, just as his father does, that she has heard nothing from Michael Doyle. But I felt that if she had heard from him she might have confided in you."

I wanted to say, if she did confide anything like that to me, I certainly wouldn't tell the police! But what I actually said was, "As far as I know she's heard nothing." I paused. "You haven't been able to learn whether or not he left aboard some ship?"

"No. Of course we have a list of all the ships that left New York harbor during the period from the day after Doyle was last seen at the Dorrance house in East Hampton until several days after John Dorrance's death. We have been in contact with each of those ships that carries wireless. The trouble is that so many tramp steamers don't have wireless. They don't have a set itinerary, either. When the captain of such a ship puts in at Charleston, say, he may intend to make his next stop Rio de Janeiro. But if a Charleston merchant has a large amount of cotton he wants to send to Bombay, the tramp steamer will head for India. It makes it very difficult."

"However," he went on, "we have made one discovery. We had thought that Michael Doyle must have driven the small motor car he had recently acquired out to East Hampton the night of John Dorrance's death. But two days ago we found his motor car in a public garage on West Fourteenth Street. The attendant said it had been there ever since September third, the day after Michael Doyle had that quarrel with John Dorrance and yelled up the stairs to Miss Dorrance that he would never see her again."

I cried, "That's wonderful! Don't you see? That must mean that after Michael left his car in that garage he went off somewhere, probably by ship, days before John Dorrance's death."

"It means no such thing, Miss Hoffsteader. It means only that if he did kill Dorrance, he got to the house that night by some other means than his motor car."

He paused to let that sink in. Then he said, "Will you be seeing Miss Dorrance soon?"

"Yes, on Saturday."

"If she does at any time tell you that she has heard from Michael Doyle, will you let us know?"

Feeling wretched, I said nothing.

"I understand, Miss Hoffsteader. You want to be loyal to your friend. But at the same time you are a law-abiding citizen. I don't think you would suppress information the police need, not for long." He stood up. "Well, goodbye."

Fortunately Amanda did not put my loyalty to the test. Neither the next Saturday nor on subsequent Saturdays when I came to the sanitarium did she tell me that she had heard from Michael. And I was sure she had not. Otherwise her eyes would not have continued to hold that despairing look.

One Saturday in early October when I was visiting

Amanda at the sanitarium, Dr. Carl Bauer also came to see her. He offered to drive me home in his new motor car, a stately Chalmers with brass headlamps.

"I'm worried about her," he said, as we drove beneath overarching trees, some of them bare now, which bordered a dirt road in Van Cortlandt Park. "She should be improving, but she doesn't even seem to want to get better. Perhaps that's understandable. It isn't just that she's lost her father and her lover. I think that no matter what she says, she's also afraid that Michael Doyle did kill her father. And if he did, then she is in a way responsible for her father's death. That would be a terrible load of guilt for anyone to bear."

He glanced at me and then said, "But let's talk of more cheerful things. You're looking very fit, Emma. Being a working girl apparently agrees with you."

"Yes, I'm enjoying it."

We did not speak again of Amanda during the rest of the drive.

I saw none of the other Dorrances during that time, but I heard about them from Amanda when I made my weekly visits to her. Mrs. Dorrance was now living alone, except for the servants, in the Fifth Avenue house. She had visited Amanda in the sanitarium only once. Lucy was enrolled at Wellesley and Larry at Harvard. I wondered what he had done with those V.M.I. uniforms.

Although Rose Shannon's visits to the sanitarium never coincided with my own, I knew from Amanda that her mother came there frequently. Thanks to the Dorrance family lawyer, Amanda had been able to arrange an allowance for Rose, a larger one than the monthly stipend John Dorrance had sent her. Rose no longer lived in that sunless flat, but in what she had described to Amanda as "a real nice place with its own bathroom" almost directly across town.

"And that awful Hank Dunkerly hasn't come back?" I asked her one Saturday in mid-October. We sat on one of the sanitarium's glassed-in porches. Through the glass we could see two gardeners cleaning away the blackened remains of dahlias struck by a heavy frost the night before.

"No, and I think she's glad, although I suppose she missed him for a while."

"I thought he might have heard she had more money now, and so had decided to come back to her."

"Well, he hasn't."

One Saturday morning in November I came to the sanitarium to find her weeping on the daybed in her pleasant room, with its chintz furniture bathed by the sunlight pouring through the wide window. "It's my locket," she said. "I don't know where it is."

"Locket? What locket?" Amanda had never been a jewelry fancier. Although she owned a number of fairly valuable brooches and necklaces, all presents from her father, she had seldom worn them.

"Michael gave it to me," she wept. "I was wearing it out in East Hampton after Papa came home from Europe, but I kept it hidden down the neck of my dress. It's a silver locket, with Michael's picture in it."

"When was the last time you saw it?"

"The night I decided to run away from East Hampton. I put the locket in my jewel box with my other jewelry, and put the box in my valise. I mean, I *think* I did. I was so upset that night that I'm really not sure of anything."

Voice breaking, she stopped for a moment, and then went on, "The day I got to Rose's she arranged for me to rent that flat below hers. I asked her to hide the jewel box somewhere in her flat. You see, Hank Dunkerly had been hanging around, offering to move furniture for me and so on. I'd seen him eyeing my valise. I felt that he'd go through my things the first chance he got."

"And so?"

"After Papa was—was killed, and I heard the police were looking for Michael, I didn't want to see or touch the locket. I felt it would hurt too much. But these last few days I've felt that I might—feel better if I wore it. And so I asked Rose Shannon to bring the box of jewelry up here."

Again she fell silent, pressing a sodden handkerchief to her face. I asked, "And did she?"

"She brought it yesterday! And the locket isn't in it! Everything is there except the one thing I want!" Again she began to weep.

"Amanda, you must have left it out in East Hampton, that's all."

"I know, I know! Maybe it's in my room. Maybe it's in the tower room."

"The tower room!"

"Yes. I realized as I was packing that I'd left my diary up there. I'd written quite a lot in it that afternoon, things that I wouldn't want anyone to read. I was so upset at the thought that I'd almost left my diary there that I can't remember what I did with the locket. Maybe

I had it in my hand when I went up to the tower room, and laid it down while I got my diary out of that table drawer. You know, the table we always played cards on.

"But oh, Emma! That locket and the picture in it are all I have of Michael. How could I have misplaced it, no matter how upset I was?"

"I don't know," I said. But even as I spoke, a possible explanation was forming in my thoughts. True, she loved Michael deeply, and yet for a few moments that night she might have felt something resembling hatred for him. To protect his father, he had turned away from her. And now she, carrying his child, was preparing to leave the house where she had spent the carefree summers of her childhood and young girlhood. Perhaps, without her realizing it, she had succumbed to an impulse to discard the locket, just as he had discarded her.

I said, "You must have left it in East Hampton. About the only other explanation is that Hank Dunkerly found the jewel box wherever Rose had hidden it. But he wouldn't have taken just the locket, and left the more valuable pieces."

She sat up and pushed her disordered dark hair back from her face. "I realize it must be out in East Hampton. But oh, Emma!" Her face twisted. "They won't let me go out there. I asked Dr. Delforth this morning." Dr. Delforth was the chief of the sanitarium's medical staff. "He said that I wasn't strong enough to go. He said that if I left here now the sanitarium wouldn't assume any responsibility, and wouldn't let me back in."

"Quite right, too," I said, looking at the shadows

under the violet eyes. "If the locket is out there it's safe enough. Just telephone the caretaker and ask him to look for it."

"Thorsen? How can I telephone him? There is no telephone in the caretaker's cottage."

"Oh, Amanda! Then write to him. Ask him to find the locket and send it to you."

"That old bluenose Thorsen has never liked me! He thinks I'm a— I mean, he wouldn't really look."

After a moment she added softly, pleadingly, "I *need* that locket, Emma. It's not just that it's all—all I may ever have of Michael. I feel so bad about having left it, so sort of—guilty."

If young Dr. Bauer was right about her, more guilt was the one thing Amanda did not need.

She would never ask Mrs. Dorrance, who had visited her only once, to get the locket for her. Rose Shannon, even if Amanda asked her to, would not want to seek admission to a house owned by John Dorrance's wife, particularly in the owner's absence. Carl Bauer spent his wintertime weekends at a clinic on the Lower East Side. He could not be asked to spend all those hours going to East Hampton and back just because of a locket.

"All right," I said. "I'll arrange with the school to take Monday off. That way I can go out there tomorrow and come back on Monday's early afternoon train."

19

Darkness was falling early now. As the station trap, drawn by a bony gray horse, carried me along Goddard Lane, a pale full moon—the hunter's moon—was already showing through leafless trees on the eastern side of the road. The driver left me before the iron gate in the Dorrance's stone wall, wheeled his vehicle around, and headed back toward the station.

As I had expected, I found the tall gates not only closed but locked. I reached up, grasped the end of a dangling rope, and pulled. Because the night was very still—no wind, and no traffic at all along the road—the clamor of the bell affixed to the lefthand gatepost was loud indeed. I waited, then rang again.

Had Thorsen already left for Sunday evening church services? I knew that every Sunday night he bicycled several miles to the Lutheran church on Montauk Highway. My impression had been, though, that he never set out as early as this. I rang again.

I was just about to brace myself for the walk back to Main Street and the one East Hampton hotel that stayed open all winter when I saw Thorsen's tall figure, lantern in hand, moving along the graveled driveway toward the gate.

He stopped a few feet away from me and held the lantern high, even though I am sure that the brilliant moonlight had already shown him who I was. "Good evening, Miss Hoffsteader."

His voice, like his square Scandinavian face beneath the thick silver-blond hair, held no warmth. I recalled how as recently as last June he had called me Miss Emma and made up a corsage for me. Now I was Miss Hoffsteader, aider and abettor of Amanda Dorrance's immoral folly.

"Good evening, Thorsen. I came out to look for something Miss Amanda left here."

He set down the lantern, took a large iron key from his pocket and unlocked the gates. He picked up the lantern. For a moment I thought he was going to let me carry the small valise I had brought with me. Then he lifted it with his free hand. In silence except for the crunch of our feet over gravel we went up the drive and climbed the front steps. He set my valise down, produced another key, and unlocked the front door. Reaching inside, he touched a switch. Light flooded down from the big chandelier in the entrance hall.

He picked up my valise and set it just inside the door. "If there's nothing else you want, I'm going to church."

Feeling a stir of resentment, I looked up into the aloof blue eyes that once had approved of me. "Thank you. I don't need anything." I stepped over the threshold. "Goodnight," I said, and closed the door.

The house seemed even colder than the late November night outside. And so strange. Through the drawing room's opened double doors I could see dust-sheeted furniture. I knew that underneath the muslin there were only long-familiar chairs and sofas. But for some reason, perhaps the silence, those white shapes seemed eerie, almost menacing. I climbed the stairs, over carpeting so thick that I could not hear my own footfalls.

I went into my room, turned on the light. Here too the furniture—armchair, dressing table, bureau—had become white shapes. The bed had been stripped to its mattress. Well, I knew where to find sheets and blankets. As soon as I had found Amanda's locket I would make up my bed. Then I would undress and get in bed and lose myself in the pages of a book. Thank heavens I had brought one with me, Thomas Hardy's *Jude the Obscure*. I would not have liked to descend through the silence to the ground floor and then along the hall to the library, passing on the way the study where I had found John Dorrance lying on the floor in his blood-soaked gray sweater.

As I stepped out into the hall I hoped I would find the locket right away, so that I could shut myself in my familiar room and lie in my familiar bed. I had expected, of course, to find the house cold and still. What I had not expected was a certain bleakness in the atmosphere.

In Amanda's room I swiftly divested one piece of furniture after another of its dust sheet. No locket lay on her dressing table or in its drawer. Swiftly I went through each drawer of the bureau. Nothing but nightgowns, underwear, stockings, and summer shirtwaists.

169

I opened the closet door. A current of air set the garments to swinging on their padded hangers. I plunged my hand into pockets of skirts, jackets, dressing gowns, a linen motor coat. Nothing. I climbed onto the dressing table bench and shifted hatboxes around on the closet shelf. Still no locket.

In the bathroom I searched vainly through the medicine cabinet and on the glass shelf that held Amanda's cologne, talcum powder, and boxes of small cakes of lemon-scented soap from England.

Then she must have left it in the tower room. I hurried along the hall, illuminated only by the refracted glow of light issuing from her room, and then climbed the narrow flight of stairs leading to the tower room door.

The door was locked.

Unbelieving, I tugged at the knob for several seconds and then gave up. I also longed to give up, for that night, my search for the locket, and seek the comfort of my bed and book. But no. I would not only keep wondering about the locket. I would be wondering about who had locked this door, and why.

Well, even though I didn't know the answer to those two questions, I did know where I could find a key to this door. There could be little doubt that Thorsen had a key to every lock on the Dorrances's East Hampton premises. More than once, passing his cottage on days so hot that he had left his kitchen door open, I had glanced inside and seen rows and rows of keys, each hanging from its hook on a rectangular board affixed to the wall, and each with some sort of handwritten label pasted above it.

What was more, even if Thorsen had locked his door tonight, probably I could get in. One day as I left the tennis court I saw Thorsen, returning from some sort of errand, place his bicycle in the rack beside the kitchen door. He had greeted me smilingly, and then reached up to take his key down from its most unimaginative hiding place, the ledge above the door.

Should I go to his cottage now and take the tower room key down from the board? Whether or not I found the locket, I would be able to replace the key on its hook within a few minutes, long before he returned from church.

True, Thorsen had as much right to privacy as anyone else. But it was not as if I planned to enter any room beside the kitchen, and not as if my reason for entering his house would be curiosity or some even more reprehensible motive.

Besides, I did not want to wait for Thorsen to come back. Already tired and tense, I did not like the thought of seeing him again tonight, that once friendly man who had turned frosty and censorious.

I went downstairs and then out the front door, first making sure that the latch was turned so that I could get back in. A wind had sprung up. As I followed the graveled path, a dry leaf scuttled ahead of me like a live thing. At the corner of the house the giant elm that rose higher than the tower room windows was now wind-stirred. The patterned shadows of its bare branches moved across the dead lawn and, around the corner of the house, across the flagstone terrace that lay beneath the tower room's east window. As I approached Thorsen's cottage, I was aware of the reflecting pool's long rectangular basin. It had been drained for the winter and now lay blue-white in the moonlight between the rows of burlap-shrouded rose bushes and the twin line of nymphs and goddesses whose white marble had taken on that same bluish tinge.

His bicycle was gone from its rack outside the kitchen. I tried the door. Locked. I reached up to the lintel's top edge and found the skeleton key.

Moonlight fell through the rectangular panes of the window onto the linoleum-covered floor and the dully shining black cookstove. I had expected to find the dangling light cord easily, but perhaps my eyes were still dazzled by the flooding radiance outside. I groped vainly in the air for perhaps a minute. Then I turned back toward the kitchen door. Perhaps in the caretaker's cottage, too, John Dorrance had gone to the extra expense of installing wall switches. I felt up and down the wall on each side of the door. Nothing.

I turned around. Moonlight filtering through the window showed me not only the stove but the wall shelf set above and to one side of it. Of course. The shelf would hold matches.

Thorsen, a tall man, had set the shelf at a height convenient for himself. Standing on tiptoe I felt cautiously along it. Yes, here was a box of matches. As I grasped the box the side of my hand brushed something cool and smooth. A second later I heard an object strike the floor. Well, no matter. It hadn't sounded as if it had broken.

I struck a match and immediately saw the light cord, dangling to a point not three feet away from me and perhaps a foot above my head. My groping fingers must have missed it by only an inch or two. I turned on the light, shook out the match flame.

As I turned to restore the matchbox to the shelf, I saw what I had knocked down. It was a small glass jar, and although it had not broken it had spilled part of its contents onto the floor—tacks, screws, small nails. And something else, something that made me stiffen with unbelieving shock.

Automatically I replaced the box of matches on the shelf and dropped the spent match in the wastebasket beside the stove. Then I bent and picked up the small oval of bright metal.

It was one half of a cuff link, initialed M.T.D. Attached to the back of it was a short length of very fine chain, ending in a tiny rod-shaped piece designed to fasten into the other half of the cuff link.

I looked down at it stupidly. How on earth had it gotten into that jar?

A memory of Poe's *The Purloined Letter* flashed through my mind. The letter that someone had hidden by leaving it in plain sight.

In that same way, the other half of Michael Doyle's cuff link had been hidden. Not in a locked drawer, or taped to the underside of a table, or sewn up in a sofa cushion, but in a glass jar left in plain sight, a jar which no one would be apt to investigate because it so obviously held the small nails and screws which any householder needs to install a towel rack or to hang a calendar on the wall.

But how had it come into Thorsen's possession? Had

173

he found it somewhere on the grounds? Yes, probably. But after John Dorrance's death, why hadn't he come forward to say that he had the other half of—

A footstep outside. A thud, as if he had not bothered to put his bicycle on the rack but had let it fall against the cottage's wall. I had time only to drop the cuff link in my coat pocket before the door opened and he stood in the doorway, filling it. His cold blue gaze went from my face to the metal objects scattered over the floor and then back to my face.

He turned, closed the door.

When he turned back toward me, I said in a voice that sounded thin and high even to my own ears, "Didn't you go to church?" Perhaps there was no reason for me to feel this panicky quickening of my heartbeats, I told myself. Perhaps he had forgotten he put the cuff link in that jar. People did forget such things. Or maybe it was someone else who had put it—

"One of my bicycle tires went flat about a mile from here. If I'd walked the rest of the way I'd have been too late for the service."

"Oh," I said in that thin, mechanical voice. Then: "Forgive me for coming into your house like this, but I thought you might be quite late. And I need the key to the tower room. The door is locked."

He nodded his still-handsome head. "About a week ago a wind storm twisted off a small branch of that big elm and sent it through one of the windows up there. Until I can get the window fixed there's always a chance of birds getting in."

His gaze again was sweeping over the small metal

objects on the floor. He took a step or two, picked up the jar, and turned out onto the palm of his other hand the few nails and screws remaining inside it. He restored the objects to the jar and replaced it on the shelf. Then he turned to me and went on, "As you've probably noticed, that tower room door comes open by itself sometimes. I didn't want to run the risk of birds getting into the rest of the house and making messes, so for now I'm keeping the door locked."

"I see." I paused and then added, "I'm sorry I knocked that jar off the shelf. I was looking for matches and—"

"Never mind." He strode past me to the key rack, attached to the wall beside the door leading into the next room. "Here." He handed me a key and then stepped through the doorway into the room beyond. "Wait there a minute, Emma."

Not Miss Hoffsteader, as it had been lately, or Miss Emma, as it used to be. I dropped the key into the coat pocket that held the cuff link. From the next room came the sound of a drawer opening and then closing.

With sudden certainty, I knew I had better not wait.

I moved to the kitchen door, grasped the knob. It turned under my hand, but the door did not open. It took me at least several seconds to realize that Thorsen, when he turned to close the kitchen door, also had shoved the little barrel bolt into place. I raised my hand to push it back.

"Don't do that, Emma. Just turn around."

I stood rigid for a moment, and then turned.

He held a gun. To this day I don't know whether it

was a revolver or an automatic. All I know is that it looked a little smaller than the ones I had seen New York policemen wearing.

Until it happens to you, you can't know what it is like to find yourself staring at the ugly mouth of a gun. Your whole body, your every nerve and ounce of flesh, seems to shrink in anticipation of a bullet's smashing impact.

He stretched out his left hand. "Give it to me."

I moved stiff lips. "Give you what?"

"You know what I mean. The cuff link. Will you give it to me, or do I have to take it?"

I fumbled with numb fingers in my pocket, found the cuff link, laid it on his outstretched palm. As he dropped the cuff link into a pocket of his heavy wool jacket, I took a step backward.

"Turn around."

"No!" I felt I must not turn my back on that gun. "Please, Thorsen. Tell me what this is all—"

"Don't pretend you don't know I killed John Dorrance. You must have known as soon as you saw that cuff link."

I had not. I hadn't had time to think things through between the moment I picked up the cuff link and the moment I heard his bicycle thud against the house wall. I stared at him. Thorsen, who had worked for the Dorrances for thirty years. How could he be the one who—

I heard myself whisper, "Why?"

His eyes took on a brooding look. After several seconds he said, "I think I'll tell you why. Yes, I'd like for you to know just how rotten a bunch you got yourself mixed up with." His face twisted. "John Dorrance ruined my little girl. She was all I had after my wife died, and he ruined her."

He's insane, I thought. Aloud I said, "But Thorsen. It wasn't John Dorrance who ran away with your daughter." I had some desperate, muddled idea that if I could convince him that he'd had no reason to kill John Dorrance, he would be less likely to harm *me*. "She ran away with a man who clerked in an East Hampton grocery store."

"Don't try to tell me about my own daughter." No madness in his face or voice, just pain and icy rage. "Oh, for a while I thought she'd been a good girl up until she took up with that grocery clerk. And I was grateful— yes, grateful!—that John Dorrance kept me on in spite of the scandal. Then she wrote to me from Philadelphia."

His bitter voice went on, describing his daughter's letter. Her lover had walked out on her, she wrote, and now lots of days she felt "sick in the head." She had no money, and wanted her father to ask John Dorrance for some.

"And then right at the end of her letter she said Dorrance ought to be willing to cough up some money, because when she was not quite sixteen he'd seduced her.

"Not even sixteen! Why, two or three years before that she had still been playing with dolls. And John Dorrance had *seen* her playing with dolls. Before that, he'd seen my wife pushing her in her baby carriage, because my daughter had lived her whole life on this place. And yet, when she was still short of sixteen—" He broke off.

I believed him. I thought of Rose Shannon saying, "Two other girls at the Haymarket had been his lady friends before he met me." It was not surprising that he'd had other extramarital adventures since Rose Shannon.

I said, trying to keep the words pouring out of him, and trying not to look at that ugly gun mouth, "Did John Dorrance give you money for your daughter?"

"Yes. Oh, not right away. He wouldn't even admit what he'd done. In fact, he never admitted it, not in so many words. But finally he said he'd give me an extra fifteen a month to send to her at this state hospital a doctor committed her to. She's still there. Sometimes her mind's all right, sometimes it isn't."

Fifteen a month to Thorsen's daughter. Fifty a month to Rose Shannon. How many other past fancies had he been paying for, that self-indulgent man who had reacted so vengefully to Amanda's moral lapse? For a moment, through my terrified awareness of the gun leveled at me, I felt a surge of anger toward the dead man.

Thorsen said, "All right. Turn around. Open the door."

I asked thinly, "What are you going to do?"

"Open the door, Emma."

"But you haven't told me why, years later— I mean, you haven't told me why you went to his study that night last September and—"

"I'm tired of talking." He suddenly looked tired, his face slackening, his wide shoulder drooping. "Go on, Emma."

"You've always liked me," I said desperately. "You know that."

"Yes, I've liked you. But you should never have stayed mixed up with the Dorrances, especially after you knew that Amanda had gone bad. Now open that door. Don't make me—"

Don't make me kill you right here. That was what he had meant. And he would kill me, unless I could think of a way to stop him. He had already proved he was capable of murder.

With a hand that felt as if it were made of wood, I unlatched the door, opened it. Aware that he held the gun only inches from my back, I stepped out into that radiant moonlight.

20

Despite my sense of unreality, as if it were only in a dream that I moved through that brightness with a gun pointed at my back, my mind was still functioning. He was a murderer, yes. But he was also a religious man, so pious that he was not content to go to Sunday morning services, but attended those in the evening as well. Surely I should be able to turn that religious feeling to my advantage.

We were moving along that flagstoned terrace at the side of the house. Ahead, striking off to the right, was the path leading to the bench where Michael and I had sat that starlit June night.

I must make him speak to me, I thought frantically. I must keep him realizing it was not just anyone moving before that leveled gun, but Emma, a girl he'd once liked and approved of. "Thorsen?"

"Yes?"

"That path leading up to the bench. Did you find the cuff link there?"

"No, on the driveway, the morning after that birthday party last June."

"It—it wasn't like you to have kept it."

"I planned to sell it. I needed money. And don't tell me what is or isn't like me. Now keep moving, and don't talk."

We rounded the corner of the house. On legs that felt numb I climbed the front steps and, at his direction, opened the front door. I had left the light on. The radiance pouring down from the chandelier seemed to have that same unreal quality as the moonlight outside. I climbed the stairs. Behind me, Thorsen said, "The tower room." I turned left, walked through the fan of light issuing from Amanda's room. With him close behind me I climbed the flight of narrow stairs to the tower-room door.

"You've got the key. Use it."

I took the key from my pocket. Only the dimmest of refracted light from Amanda's room reached the top of the tower-room stairs. Nevertheless, I managed to find the keyhole. I pushed the door back.

"Leave the key in the lock."

With that sense of moving through a nightmare even stronger now, I took a couple of steps into the room. Moonlight struck through the broken window to cast shadows on the floor, moving shadows of the giant elm's wind-stirred branches.

A click behind me. Light flooded down.

Strange, but the first thing I saw after the light went on was the silver locket. It lay on the glass-covered surface of the wicker table on which Amanda and I so often had spread out our cards for Russian bank.

Thorsen said, "Go over to the window and open it. No, not the broken one. The other one."

The one above the terrace.

I knew then what he intended. Not to shoot me. That pointed gun had been just the means of bringing me here. I was to meet death by plunging sixty feet through the moonlight to the flagstones below.

He said, as if reading my mind, "Go on, Emma. Open it. I don't want to shoot you, but I will if I have to."

I moved to the window, raised its lower pane, felt cold wind blowing against my face and body. I turned. He still stood only a few feet inside the open doorway, the gun in his hand, his blue eyes bleak. I risked a step toward him.

"Stop right there, Emma."

I stopped. My right hand clutched the back of a straight wicker chair on which I had often sat. I said, "If you kill me, people will know."

"No, they won't. You came up here and opened the window and leaned out, and you got dizzy and fell. Or maybe you jumped. Maybe you came out here from New York to do just that. Oh, people might suspect it had happened some other way, but they wouldn't be able to prove it."

I said, "You're a religious man. How could you have killed John Dorrance, let alone think about killing someone you like?"

Chill gaze still fixed on my face, he said, "You're right. I liked and respected you."

I felt a crawling sensation down my spine. He was speaking of me as if I were already dead.

"That's why I'd like to tell you how it happened. Now I'm going to lower the gun. But stand still, Emma. Very still."

The hand holding the gun lowered to his side. After a moment he said, "Early last summer I heard about this Austrian doctor. He's started this hospital in Vienna where they don't just keep people like my daughter shut up. They cure them, or at least some of them. I went to John Dorrance and asked for three thousand dollars. I figured that next time my daughter started one of those spells when she's all right in the head—her good spells, like the bad ones, can last for weeks at a time—I'd use the three thousand to take us to Austria and to keep us there while we found out whether or not that hospital could help her.

"Dorrance said that he'd think about it while he was in Europe and give me his answer as soon as he got back. But when he did get back he kept saying he was too busy to talk about it. Finally I went to his study that night. It was late, and he himself let me in when I rang. Maybe he'd have given me the money if he hadn't still been so worked up over the way his daughter had behaved. And I gather he'd had some kind of row recently with his son too. Why else should he be sending him off to a military school, the last place a boy like that would want to go?

"Anyway, John Dorrance said he couldn't afford to give me the money. Couldn't afford it! We argued, and I kept getting madder and madder. Finally he said—"

Thorsen broke off. When he again spoke, his voice had thickened. "He said that he'd been providing that fifteen a month for my daughter out of the goodness of his heart. The goodness of his heart! He said that after all the girl was crazy and no one would have believed what she had told me about him. And then—"

Again he stopped speaking. After a moment he went

on, "He said, 'And anyway, anybody could tell from the time she was thirteen that she was a born harlot.' Then he turned his back on me and pretended to be looking for a book in his bookcase. He said, 'Get out of here, Thorsen.'

"I picked up that letter opener and drove it between his shoulder blades. I pulled it out and drove it in again. Even after he fell to the floor, I dropped to my knees and went on stabbing."

For a while there was silence except for the creak of the elm branches. Beneath my fear for my own life I felt horror at the thought of Thorsen's hand rising and falling, rising and falling, as he wielded that letter opener.

He said, "Finally I realized what I'd done. I got up and just stood there, knowing that the only way out for me was to fix it so that the police would think someone else had done it. Then I thought of that cuff link, and I thought of that Doyle fellow himself, and of how everyone in the household knew that there was bad blood between him and Dorrance.

"I went to my cottage. Not by the back way, because that would take me past the cook's room, and she might be awake and even look through her window to see who'd gone out the back door. So I went out the front, leaving the door unlatched, and came back the same way, with one half of that cuff link in my hand. I dropped it onto the rug near him.

"Then I opened the safe. Over the years—I'd been with him almost thirty years!—I'd seen him open the safe often enough that I knew the combination. There was money inside. About twelve hundred dollars I found out later. I took it, and not just because it would go a long way toward taking my daughter and me to Europe. I wanted to mix up the police as much as I could, make them think if they couldn't pin it on Doyle that it had been a robbery. I wiped the safe off with my handkerchief. Then I went back to my cottage.

"There it is, Emma. It was a kind of—execution. He deserved to die. I know I'll have to stand judgement for it someday, but I'm not afraid."

Had he, this pious Lutheran, managed to convince himself that he had not committed murder? Again the thought that he might not be quite sane struck me, heightening my sense of helpless terror. Perhaps I could not hope to reason with him.

I tried to keep my voice from shaking. "I can see you had cause. And I won't tell anyone about tonight. It will just be between you and me. And now, if you'll let me go down to my room—"

He shook his massive head. "Oh, Emma, Emma! Even if I believed you, I couldn't take the chance. I've got to stay free so that I can take my daughter to Europe. As soon as Dorrance's estate is settled, I'll get the thousand dollars he left me. A thousand dollars," he said bitterly, "for thirty years of service. But at least that, plus the twelve hundred I've hidden away, and plus every other cent I can scrape up, ought to get us to Europe and keep us there for a while."

Every other cent he could scrape up. So that was why he had kept the other half of that gold cuff link. How much had he felt it was worth? Twenty dollars? Probably he had planned to sell it in Europe, where it would be fairly safe to do so.

185

And where had he hidden the twelve hundred dollars?

With an almost physically painful leap of my heart, I saw him raise the gun. "Move backward, Emma."

My hand tightened on the chair back. "No! Listen to me, listen to me!"

He took a step toward me. "Do what I say, Emma."

"You said you'd—executed John Dorrance. You said he'd deserved it. But do I deserve it? What have I ever done to you, or to your daughter?"

I saw a sudden hesitant look in his eyes. The hand that held the gun lowered slightly. Nevertheless, he took another step toward me.

I picked up the chair with both hands and flung it at his head, as hard as I could.

He must have loosened his hold on the gun, because as he flung up his left arm to protect his face from the flying chair, the gun fell to the floor and went off. Perhaps he was startled by the sound of the shot as well as by the impact of the chair against his crooked arm. Anyway, he staggered backward several feet.

No hope of scooping up that gun before he could stop me. I ran at it and kicked it through the open doorway. As I lunged forward to follow it, I heard it go off. In the narrow stairway its sound was thunderous.

I managed to get about halfway down the stairway before he caught me. Arms wrapped around my body he dragged me, twisting and struggling, back up the stairs and into the room. There on the level surface I was able to kick backward. I felt the heel of my shoe strike his shin. For a moment his grasp loosened slightly. I managed to break free, but only for a second or two. He caught me again. Facing me now, hands grasping my upper arms, he propelled me backward toward that open window.

He was a still-vigorous man half a foot taller than I and at least fifty pounds heavier. And yet—kicking at him, twisting in his grasp to sink my teeth into his hand, getting my own hand free for a moment to rake my nails down over his left eye—I managed to slow our progress across the room. Inevitably though, his superior strength would prevail. Soon I would feel the window's low sill against the back of my legs. And then there would be that long, helpless plunge down through the moonlight . . .

Until then fighting for my life, I had wasted no breath in screaming. But now, sure that I had lost the fight, I let scream after hopeless scream rip from my throat. Soon, I thought, with a strange detachment, he would fasten his hands around my throat to throttle those sounds. But he did not, and after a moment I realized why. If there were finger bruises on my throat when I was found down there on the terrace, people would never believe that I had fallen or jumped . . .

I knew that by now he had forced me to a point only a foot or two from that open window. I felt a blast of cold wind. Again I screamed.

Then, through that sound tearing out of my throat, I heard another sound—footsteps pounding up the narrow stairs.

Thorsen heard it too. Loosening his hold on me, he whirled around.

A man stood in the doorway, a man with a thickening middle-aged figure and a frightened middle-aged face.

He held a gun, a large one, in his visibly unsteady hand. After a dazed moment I recognized him. Orren Creavey, one of Goddard Lane's private patrolmen, who until tonight probably had encountered no one more dangerous than a small boy trying to sneak over a wall to explore someone's summer estate.

Perhaps Thorsen, blood obscuring his vision, did not see the gun in the other man's hand. More likely he did see it, but thought that a man like Orren would not use it. Anyway, he launched himself at the smaller man, in spite of Orren's cry for him to stop.

Orren pulled the trigger. There was a report, a louder one than those made by that other gun, now lying somewhere along the narrow stairway. I saw Thorsen spin around and crumple to the floor.

Now something was wrong with my own eyes. The room seemed filled with a thickening mist. It turned black and closed in around me.

An unmeasured interval later I came awake to find myself lying on the bare mattress in Amanda's room. Orren sat on a straight chair beside me. His gun, I noticed, had been restored to the holster strapped around his middle. As I looked up at him I saw the anxiety in his eyes lessen, but only a little.

I said, "I fainted, didn't I?"

He nodded.

"Is Thorsen—"

Orren's eyes seemed to flinch. "He was alive a few minutes ago, but I'm afraid he's pretty bad. Oh, God! For ten years I've carried a gun on this job, but I never expected to use it. And when I heard those shots from inside this house tonight, it was all I could do to make myself climb over the wall and—"

"Try not to look at it that way." I felt far too tired to talk, but I had to take that guilty look off his face. "If it hadn't been for you, he'd have killed me tonight, just as he killed John Dorrance."

"He killed Dorrance? Is that why tonight he was trying to—"

"Yes, I found out about it." I paused. "Have you called the police?"

"Yes. They're sending an ambulance, too." After a moment he added, "When the police get here, I suppose they'll want to talk to both of us. But after that . . . Well, I don't suppose you'll want to spend the night alone in this house."

I shuddered. "No."

"You can stay with my missus and me. I'm sure the police will take you to our house."

Eric Thorsen, aged fifty-three, died in the Southampton hospital that night, or rather, about three in the morning. Sergeant McNamara told me so when he came to the Creaveys' little house before noon the next day to ask a few more questions. Not that additional information from me was really necessary, except for confirmation. While he lay in the hospital, gradually weakening from an internal hemorrhage the doctors were able to slow but not stop, he had made a full confession.

He had even told the police where to find the twelve hundred dollars he had taken from John Dorrance's safe. He had dug up a young juniper, placed a metal box containing the bank notes in the cavity, and then replanted the tree.

McNamara said, "It's sad about that daughter of his. She'll have nothing and no one now."

"I think someone will send a regular allowance to her hospital, so that she can have a few comforts."

After a moment he said, "Amanda Dorrance?"

"Yes. And I imagine she'll be more generous than her father was."

He said dryly, "I think that's a safe guess." Then he asked, "Do you plan to go to New York today?"

"On the one o'clock train, if that's all right with the police."

"Perfectly all right."

I hesitated and then said, "There's one favor I would like to ask. I came out here to get a locket Amanda left in the Dorrance house. It's on a table up in that tower room, and I can't, I just can't—"

I broke off. After a moment he said, "So you want someone else to get it for you." From the way he spoke I realized that he had decided to ignore some sort of official regulation. "I'll bring it to you myself."

He looked through the window to what was apparently a brand new acquisition of the Riverhead police, a shiny black motor car with the words "Suffolk County Police Department" lettered in white on its front door. "And after that I'll drive you to the train."

21

Very soon it became apparent to me that deep within her Amanda must have feared that Michael had indeed killed her father. Once she knew he had not, her behavior changed dramatically. She regained her appetite, and her crying fits ceased. Within two weeks she was able to leave the sanitarium for the Dorrance house on Fifth Avenue.

Not that she became the Amanda she once had been. She was calm, pleasant, and perhaps nicer to know than the old Amanda, but most of the sparkle had gone.

She and I fell into the habit of lunching together on Saturdays, often at the Plaza. I talked of happenings at the Bradley School—a clash between the art and drama mistresses, or the enrollment of two of the King of Siam's daughters. Amanda talked, not of boys and parties, as she would have only a year before, but of her volunteer work. After all that had happened, she neither expected nor received an invitation to join the Junior League. As for taking a paid job, rich girls did not do that, not in those days. Instead she gave her services as an aide to professional social workers on the

Lower East Side, men and women who sought medical aid for sufferers in the fetid "lung blocks," and she toiled up mean flights of stairs to learn if the very old had coal and the very young fresh milk, and gave encouragement to the gifted boys and girls who, in amazing numbers, sprang from that neighborhood of crowded flats and overworked, undernourished people.

Now and then she spoke of Clara Dorrance, in the offhand way one might mention a fellow tenant, almost a stranger, in a large apartment house. I thought of the odd existence of those two rich women in that Fifth Avenue mansion, alone there except for servants, and yet with their lives seldom touching. Amanda lived in her world of social work and of teas and lunches with those few friends who had not turned their backs on her. Mrs. Dorrance lived in her world of theater and opera and frequent visits to Boston to see her son and daughter.

Amanda visited Rose Shannon now and then, but I gathered that no real closeness had sprung up between them. Their nineteen-year separation and the differences in their background had created a gulf too wide. Hank Dunkerly, Amanda reported, had not reappeared in her mother's life. Rose did not seem to mind. She had a new friend, a widower who ran the candy-and-newspaper store on her block.

Early in January, on a Saturday when Amanda and I had braved a snowstorm to meet amid the Plaza's warm splendor, she told me that she had been to Philadelphia.

"To see Thorsen's daughter?" I knew that she was supplying a regular amount to the hospital administration so that Amy Thorsen, during her "good" times, could enjoy such luxuries as cologne, special food, and whatever magazines she wanted. "Did you see her?"

"Yes, but she did not see me. At least I don't think she did. It was during one of her bad times. An attendant brought her into the reception room and sat her down facing me. I talked about the weather and anything else that came into my head. She just sat there, not frowning, not smiling, not speaking, just staring past my shoulder."

I really didn't want to know the answer, and yet I heard myself ask, "What does she look like?"

"She's fat now, but you can tell she was once very pretty. Blue eyes, and nice features, and hair that's still blond although there's lots of gray in it."

I thought of Thorsen in his kitchen, blue eyes bleak, gray-blond hair shining under the droplight. Then, as always when a memory of that night assailed me, I managed to push it aside.

Less than two weeks later, Amanda had news of Michael Doyle.

She telephoned me at the school that afternoon, excitement in her voice. Would I meet her at the Plaza for tea?

An hour later, while in the background a string ensemble played "Tales of the Vienna Woods," Amanda said, "Michael's father telephoned me this morning. He said he'd had a postcard from Michael from Marseilles. I asked if I could come to his office and he said yes."

A drawstring bag, made from the same brown velvet as her suit, dangled from her left wrist. From it she took a postcard. "I know Mr. Doyle likes you, Emma, so I asked if I could borrow it long enough to show it to you."

Like many postcards of that time, this one did not show a photograph of some local scene, but the painting of a flower, in this case a yellow chrysanthemum. I turned the card over. He had written:

Dear Dad,

Arrived here today after freighter trip that included several South American ports. Don't want to come home just yet so have signed onto a ship that's heading tomorrow for Baltic ports. Hope all goes well with you. Will write again.

Love,

Michael

I handed the card back to her. Her violet eyes held none of the excitement I had heard in her voice over the telephone. I felt that her first joy in having news of him had given way to other considerations.

She said, "He doesn't even say what ship he had signed onto. There's no way of reaching him."

After a moment I said, "He did that because—"

"I know. Michael didn't want to tell his father how to reach him because he's afraid I'd coax the information out of him."

"But don't you see, Amanda? That doesn't mean he doesn't love you. It's just that he doesn't know that—that everything has changed here." I meant, Michael doesn't know that John Dorrance is dead, and so no longer can harm Matthew Doyle. But I saw no need to say it aloud.

She said quietly, "Perhaps Michael still loves me. But for how long, Emma? He's so wonderful, so attractive. And he thinks that there is no chance for him and me. How long before some other girl—"

For a moment I thought of trying to say something to comfort her. Then I decided against it. The chances were that she was right. The chances were that a handsome, virile young man would not remain bound for long to a love he considered hopeless. It was good that Amanda realized that. Perhaps in time she too would respond to someone else.

I looked at the watch pinned to my jacket. "I must get home before my mother starts to worry."

To my disapproval, Amanda and Matthew Doyle struck up a friendship. Twice they lunched together. Although she did not tell me so, I knew that they must have spent ninety percent of their time together talking about the young man they both loved.

In early March, Matthew Doyle died of a heart attack in his office. An assistant found him slumped over his desk.

The newspaper obituaries made no mention of the fact that for a while the police had searched for Matthew Doyle's son as a suspect in the John Dorrance case. Perhaps the reporters were being considerate. Or perhaps it was just that the Dorrance case was no longer deemed of much interest. After all, there was much to occupy the public mind that spring, including the probability of war between the Triple Entente and Germany and her allies.

Amanda and I attended Matthew Doyle's funeral, sitting in a rear pew of a Catholic church on Manhattan's Upper West Side. In Amanda's face there was real sorrow for the warm-hearted man her father had called an "Irish saloonkeeper." But at the same time I knew she must be grieving at the thought that the one living link between herself and Michael had snapped. After we shook hands at the church door with Matthew Doyle's tall, bony sister and her somewhat shorter husband, after we had gone down the steps to the slushy sidewalk and turned to walk through a raw March wind toward Central Park West, I heard Amanda mutter, "Well, that's that."

I knew that I shouldn't encourage any hopes she might still have, but she looked so wretched that I could not help myself. I said, "Michael was his father's heir, wasn't he?"

"Yes, his only heir."

"Then Matthew Doyle's lawyer will be looking for Michael now."

"I know. I talked to him."

"The lawyer? But how—"

"As soon as I read that Mr. Doyle had died I called his office. His secretary gave me the name of the lawyer, and I went to see him. He says he'll advertise in the London *Times* and a few European papers. But I think he won't look very hard, because there can't be much of an estate, not after all the debts are paid."

Debts. Those debts represented by "the paper" John Dorrance had bought up from the original lenders. Now those debts would be paid back into John Dorrance's large and complicated estate. Strange to think that when that wealth was finally divided by Clara Dorrance and Amanda and the twins, part of it would represent the business built up by an Irish immigrant.

Easter came early that year. Because Amanda would be all alone—the twins, who had a week's recess from college, had gone with Clara Dorrance to Atlantic City— my parents and I invited her to have the traditional feast with us. At the last moment my mother also invited my cousin, Paul Miller. His father had been called to Chicago on business, and so Paul too was alone.

When I saw the stunned look on my cousin's handsome face at sight of Amanda, I wondered why I hadn't before this thought to introduce them. As for Amanda, she appeared not unaware of the admiration of this tall, blond young man. It seemed to me that some of her sparkle came back. My father must have felt the impact of that renewed sparkle, because he began to tell rather boastful stories about his undergraduate days in Germany, just as he had when I brought Amanda home for dinner during our senior year at Miss Bradley's.

Amanda and Paul saw each other frequently after that, so frequently that my Saturday luncheons with her became almost a thing of the past. She called me often though, and talked of going with Paul not only to dinner and the theater but to tea dances at various hotels, a new and increasingly popular form of entertainment. Late in May young Dr. Bauer telephoned me to suggest that he and I make up a foursome with Amanda and with my cousin, who was a patient of his, to go to "one of those tea dances at the Waldorf."

Toward the end of the afternoon Carl and I sat out a dance. The orchestra was playing a Maxixe, a fast-stepping dance from South America, which Carl said was beyond his skill. I looked at Paul and Amanda, moving expertly over the floor, and thought of that night nearly a year before when I had seen Amanda and Michael dancing at her birthday party. Paul and Amanda made just as handsome a couple, perhaps even more so because of the contrast between his blond good looks and her brunette beauty. All they lacked was that kind of radiance that had shimmered around her and Michael that night, a radiance that might have convinced the most cynical observer that in some cases a man and woman *are* made for each other, and no one else.

One Saturday afternoon in early June Amanda telephoned me. She had just been for a hansom ride in the park with Paul Miller, during the course of which he had asked her to marry him.

"Oh, Amanda! You said yes, didn't you? Please tell me you said yes."

"I said yes."

"When is it to be?"

"We haven't decided yet. Sometime in the fall."

"He's so very right for you."

He was, and not just because they made a stunningly handsome couple. Paul was a thoroughly nice young man, sensitive and generous and steadfast. Even John Dorrance, I felt, would have been pleased by this match. True, Paul and his father were not rich, but they were fairly well connected socially, and the profession of civil engineering was a respected one. I went on, "Do you realize that we'll be cousins now?"

"Yes, Emma."

"I'm so very happy for both of you."

"I knew you would be. I'm happy too, of course. I had better hang up now. Paul is taking me to dinner."

Paul came to see my mother and father and me the next afternoon. The joy in his face made me realize just how tepid Amanda had sounded when she said, "I'm happy too, of course." Well, perhaps it was usually like that. Perhaps not many couples felt an equally strong love for each other.

Only a few days later the Dorrance estate was finally settled. And a few days after that, over the phone, Amanda suggested that as soon as the Bradley School was closed, she and I should sail for Europe and spend the summer there.

I said, stunned, "But Amanda! You just became engaged. You can't go away for weeks and weeks."

"Paul and his father are going to Colorado for part of the summer. Something about a new dam. Besides, from next fall on he and I will be spending the rest of our lives together. So he doesn't mind my going."

I was sure that Paul minded very much, but I was also sure that he had agreed to her going. Probably he was too afraid of losing her to oppose strenuously anything she wanted.

I said, "I can't afford a European summer. It would take every cent I've saved from my salary."

"It won't cost you anything. I'll pay for both of us."

"You know I wouldn't let you do that."

"Please, please, Emma! Surely you see that I can't go alone."

I was gratified to learn that, even reckless and headstrong as she was, she realized that solitary European travel was unthinkable for the fiancée of a man like Paul. "You'll have to find someone else," I said.

"Who? My mother?" I knew she meant Mrs. Dorrance. "Rose Shannon? Larry and Lucy? You know there really isn't anyone else I can ask."

"I'm sorry."

"At least think about it, Emma."

At dinner that night I told my parents about Amanda's idea. My father said, "Go with her."

"But Papa. I'm saving money for teacher's college." After the amount my parents had spent on my fashionable education at the Bradley School, I took pride in the thought of paying my college expenses.

"Business has been quite good, Emma. I'll give you the money for the trip. We'll call it your twenty-first birthday present. You'll be getting it a year ahead of time, that's all."

I looked at my mother and saw doubt in her face. I knew it was not because she begrudged the money. Nor was it because she knew of Amanda's affair with Michael, or that her stay in Bellevue had been the result of more than a fall down the stairs. Thank God I had managed to keep all that from both my parents.

But there had been no way to keep them from knowing what had happened to me that cold November night I went out to the Dorrances' East Hampton house alone. Ever since then, despite her sympathy for Amanda, my mother had seemed to feel that association with the Dorrances—any of the Dorrances—might bring me ill-fortune. I had noticed, too, that her congratulations to her nephew Paul upon his engagement had been less warm than my father's.

Nevertheless she said now, "I can tell you want to go, Emma. And it's time you saw Europe."

My father said, "And we know a sensible girl like you will be safe, even if Amanda is sort of a flibbertigibbet." It was the nearest thing to criticism of Amanda I had ever heard him voice.

A sensible girl would be safe. I knew that he meant plain as well as sensible. If I had been pretty, I reflected, they would have thought long and hard before allowing me, a twenty-year-old girl, to go to Europe accompanied only by another twenty-year-old.

But no matter what their reason for permitting and even financing the trip, I felt lucky to be going. I got up from the table and kissed my mother's cheek and then my father's. "Thank you," I said.

22

We sailed the last week in June on the *Olympia*. Everytime Amanda, with me beside her, entered the dining salon, all over the room conversations died and knives and forks stopped clicking. She seemed unaware that nearly every man aboard smiled at her. To those who tried to strike up a conversation she gave the briefest possible replies. When the ship's officers, taking advantage of their status, offered to show her all over the ship, or to demonstrate with a sextant how they found the elevation of the polestar, Amanda's acceptance was polite, but nothing more than that.

A small worry I'd had subsided. Apparently she did not intend to behave in any way that I, as the cousin and friend since childhood of her future husband, would find disturbing.

We had a marvelous time during our two weeks in London. We watched the changing of the guard at Buckingham Palace, wandered through Kew Garden glades where bluebells were so thick that they looked like an azure haze over the grass, and ogled the crown jewels in the Tower. In Hyde Park one day we caught a glimpse of Queen Alexandra, widow of Edward the Seventh, who had died a year earlier. She rode in a closed carriage, looking incredibly beautiful in her black garments and with her mourning veil thrown back from her face.

In Paris, too, we did all the usual things, such as toiling dutifully through the Louvre's long corridors, and staring down into Napoleon's tomb, and struggling, bent from the waist, along the top level of the Eiffel Tower on a day so windy that we could almost feel the lofty iron construction sway.

By the time we crossed into Italy we had stopped acting as if on our return we would be quizzed by Miss Morley, our former history mistress, on Historic Sights of Europe. In Venice we did not visit the glass blowers on the island of Murano. In Florence we did not go to the Pitti Palace or visit the house where the Brownings had lived. In Rome we did not attend the Pope's public audience. Oh, we still saw many of the palaces and art galleries and museums starred in our guidebook. But we also spent a lot of time dining leisurely at sidewalk cafés, or wandering through the streets with no more definite purpose than to enjoy the foreign sights and sounds, or turning on impulse into shops or churches that were not even mentioned in our guidebook.

Everywhere we went in Italy young men and some not so young followed us. By us, of course, I mean Amanda. Sometimes they would walk along beside us for several yards, speaking softly and rapidly. I am sure that at least some of them made indecent proposals, but since they always spoke in Italian, a language neither Amanda nor I understood, no harm was done.

We decided to spend in London our last week before our boat sailed for New York. All through the long train journey north from Rome to Calais, Amanda was very quiet. Most of the time she just stared out the window at vineyards or ancient farmhouses or at distant, castle-crowned hills. For hours at a time she would speak only in answer to a question, and then only briefly.

In London we registered at the same Cadogan Square hotel where we had stayed before, a dignified hostelry which had been recommended by my employer, Miss Farnsworth. Over our early dinner that night in the almost empty dining room, Amanda said abruptly, "Let's go to Ireland tomorrow."

"Ireland! But Amanda, we were going to see Strat-ford-on-Avon, and Brighton, and Bath. Remember how I told you that for a while Jane Austen lived in Bath? We were going to—"

Then I broke off, realizing why she wanted to go to Ireland. I said quietly, "No, Amanda. Going there will just—just help keep something alive, something you must forget if you possibly can."

"But I want to go there! And I want to go to Loughglen."

The name of that village conjured up those minutes when I had sat with Michael Doyle in the starlight, and listened to him talk of the place where his ancestors had lived.

"Amanda, don't be foolish. Even if we did go there we could stay only a few hours, overnight at most. Then we'd have to come back to England. We sail for home on the tenth, remember."

"That's all I want, just a few hours." Tears in the violet eyes. "Emma, I'm going to spend the rest of my life being a good wife to Paul. Can't I have just those few hours?"

"Amanda—"

"He said it was a beautiful place." The tears were rolling down her cheeks now. "Maybe there, in that place he liked so much, I can really say—say goodbye to him in my heart. Maybe I can come away feeling at peace."

At last I said, "All right."

I said it not just because her words had touched me. I also said it because I feared that otherwise she would go without me. And I had the feeling that if she did that the result might be disastrous, both for her and for my cousin.

Leaving our trunks at the hotel, we went to Paddington Station the next morning and boarded a train which connected London with the Irish Channel port of Holyhead. It was a slow train which made many stops. Consequently we did not reach Holyhead until the next afternoon. By contrast, our passage across the channel to Dublin was both swift and smooth. As our steamer approached the docks, it moved across mirror-smooth water stained pink and gold and lavendar by the sunset.

We stayed overnight in Dublin and then took an early train south to Kilvalin. According to the map, Kilvalin was the nearest railroad stop to Loughglen. To take us the rest of the way, we hired the only form of transportation available, an Irish jaunting cart, with its two long seats running back to back the length of the vehicle. Yes, its elderly driver assured us, we would find an inn in Loughglen. It had changed hands recently. A young couple from Waterford had bought it.

So as to balance the cart and make things easier for the ancient gray horse who drew it, Amanda and I sat back to back. Thus we did not talk much as we moved through the enchantingly beautiful but obviously poverty-stricken countryside, past lakes dotted with wildfowl, past tumbledown farm huts where small ragged children in the bare yards started at us unsmilingly, past potato fields where their elders, digging up the crop, seldom paused even long enough to more than glance at us. Despite these evidences that Ireland was still a poor country, I would have enjoyed that journey if it had not been that I felt I heard in my own mind an echo of Amanda's thoughts. Had Michael ever walked down this road, sat by that lake, seen that crumbling castle on the next hilltop much as it was now, with an arc of rainbow behind it? Or perhaps my thoughts, however near her own, were authentically mine. As I have said, I remained a little in love with Michael for a long time.

After awhile the countryside began to look more prosperous. Perhaps the soil was richer here. Perhaps the land was owned by the men who farmed it, rather than by landlords who spent most of their time in Dublin or London. Whatever the reason, the houses were in better repair, the children less thin and ragged, the men and women in the fields friendlier, waving at our driver and sometimes calling out in what must have been Gaelic, because I didn't understand a word of it.

We found that the village of Loughglen appeared to share in the relative prosperity of its nearby farms. Its main street curved past whitewashed cottages of one and two stories, their roofs well thatched. We passed a wine shop and a greengrocer's and what appeared to be a general store, with a window that displayed a round of cheese, a dangling ham, and a pile of what looked like heavy white sweaters.

The inn was on the far side of the village. Except for its hanging sign out front and its large stableyard attached to one wall, it looked like any of the village's two-story cottages. Amanda paid the driver, who told us again that he would spend the night with "kinfolk" here in the village, and then pick us up the next morning to drive us back to the railroad station in Kilhaven.

A burly, pleasant-looking man of about thirty had hurried out of the inn to take our valises. His name, he said, was Sean Gilley. We followed him back into a short hall from which a box staircase rose steeply. On our right the door to a parlor stood open. A red-haired young woman sat there. With her foot she rocked a cradle. Her right hand held a darning needle, and her left a darning egg with a man's heavy gray sock stretched over it. She smiled at us.

As we climbed the stairs Amanda asked if the baby was a boy. "No, a girl," he said, with no hint of ruefulness.

On the second floor he told us that as his only guests we could have our choice of his six rooms. The inn did most of its business in the spring, he explained, when people traveled north to Dublin for the race meets, and again in the fall, when they traveled to harvest fairs throughout southern Ireland. Since all of his rooms were small, with slanted ceilings against which one could easily bump one's head, there didn't seem to be much choice. They were clean, however, and quite attractive with their braided rag rugs and hand-quilted bedspreads. We chose the ones nearest the bathroom. Yes, there was a bathroom. He told us that the former owner had installed it early in the spring, only weeks before his wife's death had decided him to sell the place. The bathroom's porcelain fixtures were in strange contrast to its ancient oak floor and equally ancient leaded windows.

"Supper's at seven," Sean Gilley said, and left us.

It was two hours later, when we went down to the dining room opposite the parlor, that we saw the painting.

Amanda saw it first. She took a couple of steps into the low-ceilinged room with its unlighted fireplace and its small tables covered with red-and-white-checked cloths, and then came to a halt. Following the direction of her gaze, I saw a picture, in an unvarnished frame that looked homemade, hanging above a table directly opposite us. It was about a foot square. From that distance I could make out only that it showed some sort of building against the deep green of a hillside.

I had never seen any of Michael Doyle's paintings, but I knew instantly that she had recognized it as one of his, or at least thought that she had. Her face was white and her eyes distended.

Together we moved across the room and stood in front of the picture. Now I could see that it showed the ruins of a building, probably an abbey. She said, "Michael painted that."

Despite my instinctive alarm, I tried to speak calmly.

"How can you be sure?" I leaned closer. "It doesn't seem to be signed, not even with initials."

"That was probably because he didn't think it was one of his best, and maybe it isn't. But it's his." Her voice was low and passionate. "He's been here, Emma, right here in this room."

"Perhaps, several years ago. He came to this village, remember, one summer while he was still in college."

"He's been here since then! Just months ago, or weeks, or even days. I know it!"

Sean Gilley, with a white apron tied around his middle, came into the room from what must have been the kitchen. "Will this table suit you, ladies?"

He pulled out chairs for us. When we were seated, Amanda asked, "Who did that picture?"

He looked curiously down at her tense face and then said, "Pretty, isn't it? That's the old abbey in Glen Wicklow, a few miles from here. The former owner—Sullivan, his name was—was going to take it with him, but my wife and I liked it, so he left it here. No, I don't know the name of the artist. Sullivan just said that the painter was a young American who'd come up here from Cork. He hadn't liked the picture much and had been about to throw it away. But Mrs. Sullivan asked if she could have it, so he gave it to her."

Amanda's eyes, blazing with excitement and triumph, looked into mine. I turned to Sean Gilley. "When was the painter here? Several years ago?"

He shrugged. "I couldn't say. We've been here only three months. Could have been as late as last May, just before we took over. Now I hope you'll enjoy your supper, ladies. My wife made beef pie."

When he had gone back into the kitchen Amanda said, "Michael came here a second time. He saved his money from his wages on that ship that took him to Marseilles and from the one that took him to the Baltic. Maybe he signed onto another one that brought him to Cork. Anyway, he came to Loughglen and stayed at this inn—"

Gilley came into the room, carrying a tray laden with two glasses and a pitcher of water. When he had returned to the kitchen I said, "Amanda, you can't know that he was here recently instead of years ago. Anyway, he's not here now, so what difference does it make? And tomorrow you and I are going back to Dublin, and from there to London, and from there—"

She said, as if I hadn't spoken, "His father came from here! Probably there are still Doyles in this village, and Michael visited them. They must know where he went."

Gilley came in with two steaming plates, each bearing a slice of beef pie. When he had set the plates down Amanda asked, "Are there any people named Doyle in this village?"

"Not any longer, except in the graveyard. Lots of them there. But I guess some of the Doyles went to America or England or Australia, and the rest of them just died out. Anyway, I know every soul in this village, and there are no Doyles."

Amanda asked, in a taut voice. "Where is the former owner of this place?"

Again Gilley gave her that curious look. "Sullivan? He went to America to be with his son. I can't rightly say just where. Not New York. Chicago, or Boston, or

Detroit, or one of those places. Anything more you want right now, ladies?"

We both told him no. When he had gone I said, "You see? There's no way of finding out. Now when we get to Dublin tomorrow afternoon—"

"There are ways! Probably he stayed at a hotel in Cork. In cities that size hotels keep proper registers. There'd be a record of when—"

"Amanda! You're coming home with me! If you don't, if you go off on a wild goose chase, if you do this wicked, cruel thing to Paul, then I never want to see you again or even hear from you."

My furious gaze and her stubborn, excited one locked for several seconds. I said, "I mean it, Amanda."

After a while her gaze dropped. She said in a subdued voice, "You're right. I probably couldn't find him. And even if I did . . ." Her words trailed off. Then she said, "All right. We'll go to Dublin tomorrow, and then England, and then home."

I have no doubt that the beef pie was excellent. Anger, though, had taken away my appetite. I ate only half the food on my plate, and Amanda scarcely touched hers. When Gilley showed his disappointment at our neglect of his wife's cooking, Amanda explained, quite falsely, that the jaunting cart driver had stopped at an inn that afternoon, and that we'd had tea and sandwiches there. Furious with her only minutes before, I found myself liking her again for assuaging the man's hurt feelings. We climbed the stairs, exchanged rather stiff good nights, and went to our separate rooms.

Despite my fatigue after the long day of travel, I lay

awake for hours that night listening to the silence. No sound from downstairs or from Amanda's room on the other side of the bathroom. On this windless night there was not even the stir of tree branches outside. Finally I fell asleep.

We had asked Sean Gilley to call us at eight in the morning. I awoke with a sense that it was earlier than that. The watch I had placed on the bedside table confirmed that it was only a little past seven-thirty. Nevertheless, I decided to get up. Wearing a robe over my nightdress, and with a towel over my arm and toothbrush and toothpaste in hand, I went into the bathroom. By the time I emerged I knew it must be almost eight o'clock, and so I went to Amanda's room and knocked on the door.

No answer. I knocked again. Then, feeling a sick premonition, I opened the door.

The first thing I realized was that the bed had not been slept in, although she must have lain down on it for a while because there was a dent in the pillow. I stepped into the room and looked around the wide-boarded oak floor and into the closet. Her valise was gone.

It was when I turned away from the closet that I saw the envelopes propped against a pair of pewter candlesticks atop the tall bureau. Stomach knotted with sorrow and anger, I took them down. One envelope, sealed, bore Paul's name. The other one, unsealed, was addressed to me. I dropped the sealed letter onto the quilted counterpane and opened my own note. She had written:

I know that it is no use to ask you to forgive me for what I'm doing, not when you are so fond of Paul. And so all I ask is that you try to understand.

I have to try to find him, Emma. Perhaps, if I hadn't seen that painting— But I did see it, and now I have the feeling that he may be somewhere quite close, perhaps in Cork. Anyway, perhaps I'll learn something about him there. And if I can't, I will hire people to try to find him.

You won't have to explain anything to Paul. Just give him the letter I've written. It's all in there.

By the time you read this, I will have left Loughglen. I said I was not going to ask you to forgive me, but I do ask it, Emma.

She had signed it, "Affectionately, as always, Amanda."

With fingers that shook, I tore her letter into tiny, tiny pieces and dropped them into the wastebasket beside the bureau. I had a strong desire to tear up her letter to Paul also, but of course I did not. I put it in the pocket of my robe and left the room.

Sean Gilley was emerging from the staircase into the upper hall. He said, "I was just coming to call you."

I knew that even though I was clad in dark blue flannel from my chin to my toes, convention demanded that I not carry on a conversation with a male while I was wearing a dressing gown. But I was too upset to care about convention. Instead of dodging quickly into my room I said, "Miss Dorrance has gone?"

"Yes." I became aware of the frank curiosity in his face. "When I got up this morning to start the fire in the stove I found her sitting on a chair just inside the front door. That was a little after six o'clock. She asked me if I knew anyone in the village who would drive her to Cork for fifty dollars. I told her I knew several who would drive her all over Ireland for that much."

"So you did find a driver?"

"Yes, I asked Flaherty, the blacksmith. Like a shot he said he'd pick her up in his trap in half an hour. When I got back here from the blacksmith's I saw she must have been up to her room, because she was just coming down the stairs."

In her room, I thought, writing those letters.

"I asked her if she wanted breakfast, and she said just tea. Then she asked me not to call you until eight." He paused. "Will you be wanting breakfast?"

"Yes," I said crisply, "and soon, please. I'll be leaving for Dublin at nine."

23

In London I told the hotel manager that Miss Dorrance's plans had "changed."

"But her trunk, Miss Hoffsteader. You will be taking
that to Southampton with you tomorrow?"

"No. I imagine she will send for it later." I wondered
if she really would or if, twenty years from now, it would
still stand in the hotel storeroom, gathering dust.

While I ate my solitary meal that night in the stately
hotel dining room, surrounded by English people who
seldom raised their voices above a murmur, I wondered
if I might make it easier on both Paul and myself by
cabling him the news. But I could not think how to
phrase a cable telling a man that the girl he expected to
marry had gone off looking for her ex-lover.

Besides, there was the chance that she would come to
her senses soon, or perhaps already had. In that case she
would send him a cable saying that she would be home
on a later ship.

But when, on a morning eight days after that, the
Olympia moored at its Hudson River berth, I wished
fervently that I had sent him that cable. He was down

there in the crowd on the dock, eyes eagerly scanning the line of passengers at the ship's rail.

His gaze found me. After a moment his expression changed. Even though more than a hundred feet separated us, I could see that he had turned white.

As soon as I stepped onto the dock he caught my arm. "Where is she? Did she take sick? Is she still—"

"Nothing like that. She wrote a letter." I reached into the pocket of the heavy wool coat I had donned on this unseasonably cold day and brought out the envelope. From the way his pale face tightened as he took it, I knew he already realized what sort of letter it must be.

He said, in a constricted voice, "I'll meet you outside the customs shed and take you home."

The ship had sailed from Southampton with almost every cabin filled. Thus it took me nearly an hour to get through customs. When I finally followed a luggage-laden porter from the customs shed to the street, Paul was waiting for me in a hansom cab. Even though he was still white, he managed to smile at me.

As the cab carried us across town, I said, "Oh, Paul! I'm so sorry, so sorry!"

He patted my hand. "I know you are. But then, I always felt it was too good to be true. That she'd marry me, I mean."

"I'm glad you can be so understanding. I can't!"

"I understand what she's done because she told me all about Michael. I know she loved him as much as I love her. If I thought I could have her, nothing or no one could stop me from trying to find her. That's how she feels about Michael."

"Then she had no right to promise to marry you!"

"Maybe she thought she could get over loving him, and then found she couldn't."

"I don't care what excuses you make for her. I'd like to wring her neck."

Instead of answering, he squeezed my hand and then withdrew his own. We rode the rest of the way to Brooklyn in almost complete silence.

A week later I went back to work at the Bradley school. And three months after that I received a Christmas card from Amanda. The envelope had the return address of a Cork hotel. The card made no mention of Michael. Below the picture of a trumpet-blowing angel she had written, "I hope all goes well with you. Love, Amanda."

Perhaps she was waiting in Cork because she had reason to think he might be coming there. Or perhaps she had found no trace of him, and remained there merely because she could not think of what else to do.

The return address on the envelope was a clear invitation for me to write to her. I didn't do so. I was still too angry. I went on being angry, even after Paul Miller in late May became engaged to a third cousin of his on his father's side, a quiet, pretty girl whom both he and I had known since childhood.

And then, some months later, I realized I was no longer angry. I began to think, not of the way she had trampled on my cousin's feelings, but of her many kindnesses and generosities, not only to me, a German immigrant's daughter with a plain face and a funny name, but to others as well. I wrote to her at that hotel in Cork, but the letter came back, stamped, "Addressee

Unknown." Reluctant as I was to renew my acquaintance with Clara Dorrance, I began to think of inquiring from her about Amanda. Then, one Saturday afternoon, I saw Mrs. Dorrance standing a few feet away from me at the glove counter in Lord and Taylor's.

When I suggested that we go somewhere for a cup of tea, she hesitated, and then consented. Perhaps she was afraid that if she refused I might start asking questions about Amanda right there in the crowded store.

We went to a tea shop on East Thirty-fifth Street and sat at an isolated table. She had received only one communication from Amanda, she said. "A few days before she was to arrive from Europe, she sent me a cable saying she had decided not to return just yet." Mrs. Dorrance offered no explanation as to why she had not telephoned me to try to learn why Amanda had remained abroad. All I could conclude was that she felt that the less she had to concern herself with her adoptive daughter, the better.

"And you have not heard from her since?"

"Not directly. Some months ago our lawyer told me that he had received a request from Amanda to transfer all of her share of my husband's cash estate to a bank in London. Later on, when the New York and East Hampton houses are sold, he will send her share of that money also to the English bank."

"You plan to sell both houses?"

"Yes, and move to Boston, so that I can be near Larry and Lucy. They have two years of college left, you know."

I suspected that she had decided to move to Boston for more reason than to be near her children. Perhaps her social position, too, had suffered because of the notoriety following her husband's death. I said, "Do you know the name of the English bank to which her lawyer transferred her money?"

She told me the name. "But I am sure they would not give you her address. Banks don't divulge such information about their depositors."

"If you hear from Amanda, will you let me know?"

After a moment she said, "Very well." But I felt she would not let me know. She wanted to have as little as possible to do with anything or anyone connected with Amanda.

She settled her fur scarf around her shoulders. "I really must leave now, Emma. I have an appointment."

I was halfway home to Brooklyn that afternoon before I thought of Rose Shannon. I doubted that Amanda had written to her. It was Amanda's lawyer who saw to it that Rose received her monthly allowance. Still, Rose might possibly have heard from her. I had never known the exact address of Rose's new flat, but as soon as I reached home I looked, without much hope, in the phone book. To my surprise, Rose Shannon was listed at an address near Gramercy Park. Her allowance from Amanda must be even more generous than I had thought if she could afford, not just a flat in a nice neighborhood, but also the luxury of a telephone.

The next day, Sunday, I telephoned her and then went to see her. She looked actually younger than when we had last met. She admitted me to a living room filled with new-looking furniture—bright floral carpet, blue overstuffed sofa and armchair, little tables filled with knickknacks. The only thing I recognized from that ghastly place in Hell's Kitchen was the kewpie doll on the mantel of the fireplace—a real fireplace, here.

A man got up from the sofa as I came in. She introduced him as Mr. Fratanelli, "who has the candy store on the corner." After a moment she said, almost shyly, "Tony and I took out a marriage license yesterday."

"I congratulate you both," I said, and meant it. Tony Fratanelli, short and bald and perhaps fifty, was no storybook hero. But he had a wonderfully sweet smile. And the expression in his brown eyes as he looked sidewise at Rose told me that he considered her the most desirable woman alive.

When we all three had sat down, Rose said, "I can offer you tea." She added, somewhat primly, "Tony and I don't use spirits."

"Thank you, but I can't stay long. I came to find out if you'd heard from Amanda recently."

Her face lit up. "Not straight from her. She's somewhere in Europe now, you know."

"Yes. We went over there together about a year and a half ago, but she stayed there." After a moment I said, "What do you mean, you did not hear from her directly?"

"It was through her lawyer. He said that she'd decided that instead of giving me an allowance each month it might be better to turn over a lump sum." She added, in an almost reverent voice, "The lawyer gave me twenty thousand dollars."

I too was impressed. Twenty thousand dollars was a great deal of money.

"For a while Tony and I couldn't decide what to do

with it except put it in the bank. But now we've made up our minds. He's going to sell his candy store, and we're going to take his money and the twenty thousand to California. Tony's brother grows oranges out there in San Gabriel Valley. With the money we've got we can buy hundreds of acres there."

I left a few minutes later. As I moved along the sidewalk through the first snowfall of the season I reflected that Amanda was breaking her links with America and with everyone connected to her former life one by one. She had transferred her money to England. She had settled on Rose Shannon a sum large enough to provide for her for the rest of her life. No doubt she had made similar provisions for that poor girl in a Pennsylvania State Hospital.

Nevertheless, perhaps she would send me a card again this Christmas.

She did not.

Over the next few months I often thought of writing to her in care of that English bank Mrs. Dorrance had mentioned. Surely they would forward my letter to her. But I had a feeling—perhaps induced by my failure to respond to her Christmas card—that Amanda had decided that she wanted to break every link with her past, including the one represented by me. And so I temporized, and more months passed in which I neither wrote to her nor heard from her.

As the months turned into years and the years into decades, I thought of her less and less, but I still did not forget her entirely. I would wonder every once in a while if she eventually found Michael, or if she was happily married to someone else, or if, like some other rich American women, she was drifting around Europe from city to city and lover to lover. I did not forget Michael either, entirely. Sometimes looking in an art gallery window I would wonder whether or not he had given up painting. Certainly he had not become an artist famous enough to be known to the general public.

But during the long stretch of years so much happened in my personal life and in the world at large—two world wars and revolutions galore and men traveling into space—that I only seldom thought of my girlhood friend.

And then six months ago, through my youngest and favorite grandson, I had news of her.

That's right, my grandson.

Yes, I had my own love story, after all. And a very exciting and satisfying one it was, no matter how unlikely that might appear to outsiders. It was a long romance, too. Carl—yes, it was "young Dr. Bauer" I married—lived long enough for us to celebrate our fifty-third wedding anniversary.

But as I said in the beginning, this is not my story. It is Amanda's. And thanks to my grandson, I know how it came out.

Datelined Paris, his letter read:

Dearest Gran,
    I'm here in France after backpacking for five weeks all over the British Isles. I liked Scotland best, but it's Ireland I want to write to you about, or rather, the village of Loughglen. I went there because of all the stories you've told me about the days before you'd even married Grandy, the ones I liked best were the ones about you and your friend Amanda. I know it

sounds crazy, but sometimes I think I used to be a little in love with her, just from looking at the pictures of her you showed me and hearing you talk about her.

Anyway, I went to Loughglen. And Gran, guess what? That inn you described is still there. And so is the painting! The moment I saw it I was sure it was the same one, a landscape of a ruined abbey at the foot of a hill.

I stayed there a week, long enough to get acquainted with the people who run it now, a couple named McLaren. His mother lives with them. Her name is McLaren too, of course, but she told me that her maiden name was Gilley and that she'd spent her whole life at the inn.

I told her about you and Amanda stopping there that September of 1911, and how Amanda had slipped away in the early morning to look for the man she was in love with. Mrs. McLaren said, "I wouldn't remember that. I was still in my cradle then."

A little while later Mrs. McLaren came to me and said, "I've been thinking. Maybe I do remember the young woman who ran away, and the man she was in love with, too!"

She told me then how in 1918, when she was almost eight, a young couple came to stay at the inn. The First World War was still on then, and the man wore a khaki uniform. They arrived in a motor car so big and shiny that she found it downright awesome, and they "talked funny." Her father—Sean Gilley, she says his name was—explained to her that they were Americans, even though it was a Royal Air Force uniform that the man wore.

"They were both so beautiful," Mrs. McLaren said, "that I hung around them as much as my mother would let me. They both had dark curly hair. And the lady's eyes were the color of purple pansies."

Mrs. McLaren can't remember how she first learned that the man in uniform had painted the picture, but she does remember seeing him and his wife as they stood before the picture one day, holding hands. The little girl asked the man if he made pictures for a living, and he laughed and said, "No, I found out I'm not that good. Right now I fly planes for a living. After the war, I'm going back to selling them." The child asked where he would get the planes and he told her that a man he knew in England was making private planes before the war and would go back to making them soon. "Just wait," he told her. "By the time you're grown up quite a few people will be flying their own planes."

Then he smiled at his wife and said, "Shall we buy this picture?" And she said, "Oh, no! Think of what it did for us, just by hanging here on the wall. Let's leave it here."

As nearly as Mrs. McLaren can remember, they left the next day.

That's all of it, Gran. No, come to think of it, Mrs. McLaren did say one other thing that struck me. She said, "It wasn't just that they were so very good-looking. When they were together there was this kind of—shimmer about them, almost as if what they felt for each other made a kind of light inside them."

Well, I thought you'd like to known, Gran. I'll be seeing you soon. No room in a backpack for presents, so I've been mailing them as I went along. If you haven't already done so, you'll be getting a Spode teacup from England and a small Waterford glass bud vase—I couldn't afford a big one—from Ireland.

Love,

Timothy

Well, there it is. Yes, I know. It's not conclusive. It could have been some other couple who lingered in that young child's memory. Many soldiers, on brief leave from that terrible war, must have brought their wives to Ireland for a few days. Maybe the man in the R.A.F. uniform was just teasing her when he let her think he had painted the picture. Some adults do enjoy imposing upon a child's gullibility. As for the wife's having eyes "the color of purple pansies," that sort of eyes are rare, but not unique.

But I think it was Amanda and Michael whom that little girl saw at the inn with that "kind of shimmer about them." I don't know how long it had taken Amanda to find him. Perhaps a year, or two or three years, or even more. But find him she did.

That is what I want to believe, and that is what I do believe.